M
T
L

The Unchosen

The

NAN GILBERT

Unchosen

HARPER & ROW, PUBLISHERS   *New York, Evanston, and London*

With thanks to

. . . Gay, for a memory

. . . Bruce, for time and skill

. . . Joyce, for research

6638

One

To go way, way back the problem began, I've often told my-self, with my name. Ellen. Ellen Frazer. What can you do with a name like that? It's as stiff and proper and old-fashioned as a nosegay of four o'clocks and bachelor's buttons. No catchy nickname. No romantic allure.

Now if it had been Elaine—ah, there's an evocative name! Elaine, the lily maid; Elaine of Astolat. Gallant knights in armor squiring gentle ladies more fragile than the shimmery veiling of their wimples. Who wouldn't be lovelier with a name like Elaine?

Or Elin. Spelled that way, the word was instantly dark

and fey and Irish, limning a creature of moods and mystery, of bright flashing temper and passionate sweetness.

But Ellen—ugh. The proper label for a leaf-dry maiden aunt or a stiff, starched nanny watching her little charges in the park.

Occasionally, when I was very young, I'd nerve myself to sign a school paper with one of those variations, but then I always erased the signature in furious haste. To let it stand —to let it be seen by the teacher, by the students who passed the paper to the front of the room—was to admit I wanted to be something more exciting than plain, blunt, stolid Ellen Frazer. And I'd never do that. You can stand almost anything —teasing, laughter, even not being noticed at all—as long as no one knows it bothers you. I learned early to keep my feelings locked inside me in a very private world where nobody, but *nobody,* was allowed in.

Not even Debbie and Kay.

Debbie Fuller and Kay Nicholson had become my very best friends way back in junior high. Looking at us you might wonder how it happened, for we were about as different as three girls could be. I was awkward and pudgy, with dark hair and pale blue eyes and too-big mouth and apple-dumpling cheeks.

Debbie outweighed me by ten pounds, though she was inches shorter (sometimes I took great comfort from that), but on her it looked different. She was like a big doll, with her flaxen hair and round, bright, slightly protruding blue eyes and pouting mouth.

And both of us were better-looking than poor Kay with her thousands of freckles and sort of orange hair. Kay was always trying to shrink herself down to a less noticeable level; she wore flats and mousy colors, and she ducked her head till it appeared to be growing forward from her shoulder blades.

But what Kay lacked in looks, she made up in brains. That girl was smart! Debbie might scream with ecstasy over a C average; my own grades bobbled unpredictably between straight A's in English to who-knows-what-next in math; but Kay was *always* on the honor roll. She was so broodingly intense about it that she practically broke out in a rash before every report card appearance, sure that this time her grades had nosedived for a fatal crash.

Yet different as we were—in appearance, in interests, in families—we had become a practically indissoluble trio, united mostly, I guess, by the need for self-defense. We three were the have-nots, leagued against the haves. The left-out pretending not to envy the soughtafter. Three high-school seniors who had never had a single date, not one—can you imagine it?

The Unchosen. In my private world that's what I called us, but of course I didn't say it aloud. To give a name to our forlorn state, even as a joke, would be hitting below the belt, breaking the unwritten rule that said wallflowers must never, never appear to notice their exclusion or to care the least bit in any event.

I felt awfully lucky having Kay and Debbie as friends. How grim if I'd had to sit alone on the school bus, walk alone through the halls of John Easton High, be the only one ignored when parties were planned, committees formed, representatives chosen! Bad enough as it was to weather such occasions, face set in a small stiff smile that made my cheeks ache, glazed unseeing eyes not quite meeting another's glance. At least as a trio our individual aloneness wasn't quite so conspicuous.

Outside of school the three of us got together often,

usually at my house because Debbie shared a room with her younger sister and Kay's house was too apt to be electric with tension, like an arena when the boxers are sparring for an opening. But my room was a secure and silent hideaway, as inviolate as a monk's cell. Even Mother didn't come in without being asked.

"That's one thing you can say for your family," Kay and Debbie often pointed out. "You can walk out of here in the morning, close the door, and know it won't be opened till you come home. Now at my house—" And they would sigh and shrug in resigned acceptance of their lot.

"I couldn't stand it," I said—and I meant it passionately, "if I thought anyone would come in while I was gone and touch my stuff. Or even *look* at it."

"How can you stop 'em if it's their room, too?" Debbie asked.

"Or if they're just plain nosy," Kay said darkly.

And then for a little while we would brood in silence, thinking of our families and the problems they presented.

I guess I was the luckiest (certainly Debbie and Kay thought so), in spite of Mother's being such a handicap. I mean, if Mother had been a smart, up-to-date career woman, for instance, or somebody with lots of social flair like Ann Allison's mother, she would have known the proper buttons to push to get a daughter off the launching pad. After all, Ann was no Miss America either, yet she had started dating in junior high. Mrs. Allison simply made a point of knowing the parents of every eligible boy; they belonged to the same clubs, met at the same parties, and went into a huddle over tea and Ry-Krisp before any school function to make sure none of *their* brood was left sitting home with a good book when the music started.

Parents in that crowd *knew* how important it was for a girl to be popular. But *mine*—

"Dating—at your age?" Dad would have said, if I'd ever mentioned it to him as a problem (which of course I didn't). "Ridiculous! Plenty of time for that later."

And if I'd reminded him that I wasn't fifteen any longer, or even sixteen—he kept forgetting—it wouldn't have made any difference. He'd have just given me a hug and said, "What's the matter, honey? Tired of being Dad's girl?"

As for Mother—well, her face would have puckered with distress, like an apple left too long in the refrigerator, and she would have immediately baked something even more caloric than usual, like a four-layer chocolate cake with heaps of fudge frosting, then cried, "Look now what I've done! We can never eat it all. Ellen, maybe you could call up a friend or two and invite them to share it with us."

"Mother," I'd told her patiently time and time again, "everybody I know, practically, is on a diet. You just don't understand; things are *different* now."

You see, Mother came from one of those little German communities back East where time almost stands still. Though she was born in the United States, you'd sometimes think she was just over from the Old Country. A soft round dumpling of a woman, smelling of good things to eat —as though maybe her talcum was a mixture from the spice cupboard, and her cologne pure vanilla extract. Mother was never so happy as when she was feeding somebody; in her credo, food was the answer to *every* problem.

That was great stuff in my brothers' day. I was only a grade-schooler when Robbie and Dan graduated, but I still remember the raft of boys that used to come home from High with them—practically the whole football team, it

5

seemed. Whooping and yelling. Sniffing delightedly as soon as they got in the door.

"Hey! Get a whiff a' that!"

"Fresh *apfelkuchen,*" Mother might say, beaming at them as if they were all her own. Or maybe it was thick crumbly cookies with a hidden heart of rich date-nut filling. Or coffee cake with streudel topping.

If I'd been closer to my brothers' ages, I'd have had it made—imagine a house teeming with big-shouldered lettermen! But no, I had to live those man-filled years between the stupid ages of five and nine. When the time came that I could have found better uses for my brothers' friends than as ball tossers or doll carriers, they'd vanished, as some poet said, like "the snows of yester-year." Leaving me no way into a world that could be defined algebraically as "girl plus boy equals whee!"

A brooding loner. A tongue-tied sideliner. An Ellen-person —pure, prim, stiff, and old-fashioned. One of the Unchosen.

Not a joyous category to be in, even when you *didn't* say the name out loud. This is what it did to Debbie and Kay and me. This is what we did about it.

Two

"Ellen!" Mother called after me anxiously. "Take your sweater now! It's a cool day."

I walked a little faster toward the gate, pretending not to hear. In Mother's girlhood she'd been practically sewed into long woolies every September; she still couldn't get used to habits of dress that permitted bare arms and legs on a fall day.

"Ellen!"

Oh, grief, here she came! I wouldn't put it past her to follow me clear to the bus stop in her apron and house slippers and that ridiculous frilled cap she wore over her curlers.

"Mother, it isn't cold. I'll look like an idiot, wearing a sweater."

"Just over the shoulders," she coaxed, rising on tiptoes to put it around me. "There now."

She lingered, smiling a little worriedly, with that don't-be-mad expression I knew so well. With an ounce of encouragement she would even give me a smacking good-bye kiss, right in plain sight of any passer-by. I opened the gate hastily.

"Got to run. Think I see the bus coming. G'bye."

Once outside the gate, though, I dawdled at turtle's pace, waiting for Kay and Debbie to appear. Even on rainy days they walked over to catch the school bus at my corner; that way we avoided even a few minutes of solitary sitting or having to share a seat with someone we didn't know very well. And that description fitted just about the whole overcrowded membership of John Easton High.

An escaped criminal, I've often thought, could have hidden out in Easton for *years,* and nobody would have been the wiser. He could even have attended classes if he'd wanted to. The town was finally getting around to building a second high school, but the decision had come too late to affect us. Our high-school days would end as they had begun—in a mob scene straight out of an old Cecil B. DeMille movie.

"Hey, wait!" Kay called. She came loping across a vacant lot, glancing at her wristwatch as she neared me. "I figured out a new shortcut. Saved me almost a minute."

The extra minute had obviously not been spent on herself. Her blouse was misbuttoned and half hiked out of her skirt; one shoelace was dragging; her glasses were speckled.

I sighed with the mixture of affection and exasperation that her appearance always roused in me. "How could you tell it was me?" I asked.

"Why, I'd know that red sweater a block away!" Kay said in surprise. Then the message got through; she took off her glasses and frowned at the speckles. "Now where did they collect all that goop? I'm sure I cleaned them this morning. Or was it yesterday morning?"

As she fell into step beside me, she polished the glasses on a fold of her skirt. The skirt was a pleated sheer wool in a muted shadow-plaid that practically begged aloud for a bright accenting color; but Kay had killed it dead with a mouse-brown blouse.

"Isn't that a new skirt?" I asked. "Looks like a Pendleton."

Kay nodded, glowering at the smeary blur that now replaced the speckles on her lenses. "Aunt Bel sent it from Portland—a sort of beforehand birthday present. I'd a lot rather have had the money. I'm having a terrible time saving up Midge's stud fee."

"Don't be silly. Your mother won't let you breed Midge anyway."

Kay's face took on a familiar mulish expression. She retorted stubbornly, "Once it's done, it's done."

It was an old discussion. We'd worn a path around it in the year since a neighbor family, moving away from town, had presented Kay with their wire-haired terrier. That dog kept Kay absolutely penniless; her mother was dead-set against having animals around the house, and wouldn't donate so much as a table-scrap to its care.

"Take that dirty thing out of here!" she'd shrieked the day Kay brought Midge home (at Kay's request, I'd gone along with her, but even with me there, Mrs. Nicholson had blown her stack). "Oh, my goodness, there'll be dog hair over *everything,* and I just finished cleaning! Get it *out,* do you hear me?"

9

The Nicholsons' house was much handsomer than ours. They had deep-pile velvety rugs I was scared to step on, and needlepoint chair backs I didn't dare lean against. Even in Kay's room, I felt uneasy, as though I'd wandered into a stage setting ("Scene: Teen-age Girl's Bedroom") and might disturb the props if I touched anything. Like the other rooms, it appeared to be lifted straight out of *House Beautiful*—all dainty pink and ivory, with frills and bows, satin pillows and long-legged dolls, and a nylon-furred turquoise monkey that Kay hated but that her mother insisted was required as an accent. In a house like that I could halfway understand why Mrs. Nicholson was upset at Midge's appearance.

But Kay had a temper to match her hair; she dug in her heels and thrust out her jaw and squared away in defense of the pooch. "The dog's mine and I'm going to keep her!"

"Not in the house, you aren't!"

"I'll fix up a place in the yard."

"Be sure it's the *back*yard and see that the dog stays there! If I catch you sneaking it into the house—just once—I'll call the pound!"

The yelling embarrassed me dreadfully, though Kay accepted it as a part of normal home life. That's why Debbie and I didn't go over to Kay's much; while ordinarily Mrs. Nicholson was very gracious in a worried, darting sort of way, we could never tell when Kay would strike sparks and provoke an explosion. Kay wouldn't soft-foot it around an issue, as Debbie did all the time—or just shut up and hope it would blow over, like me; no, whenever there was a difference of opinion, she came out with her side—bam, pow— like an orange-haired knight flinging down a gauntlet. I couldn't decide whether that was admirable or just plain dumb.

"Hi!" Debbie called. "Don't go so fast!" She came hurrying down a gravelly side road on the ankle-turning spike heels she wore with any costume on the theory they made her legs look slimmer.

"Gee," she said breathlessly, "I thought I was late. I didn't even take time for breakfast." She had a gooey caramel-nut sweet roll in each hand, and was gripping her books to her sides with her elbows. "Grab 'em quick, will you? No, no, the books—they're slipping."

Kay and I relieved her of her load. She sighed deeply and bit into a roll.

"Forgot to set the alarm again. Or Polly did. Anyway, it didn't go off."

"Thought you'd given up sweets," Kay said. "Those rolls look awfully caloric."

"Well, what do you want me to do? Starve?" Debbie protested. "I couldn't very well lug a bowl of bran flakes. Anyway, I've about given up that screwy diet. Look how long I've been on it—weeks and weeks!—and I haven't lost so much as a pound."

Kay, who had a brain for statistics like an IBM computer, said, "Eleven days."

"Eleven days *what?*"

"Since you went on your diet."

"Oh, you're crazy! I started way back before—"

"September 4th." Kay pursued an objective as relentlessly as a bloodhound snuffling a scent. "I remember because it was right after registration. We went down to Pete's for sodas to celebrate not having to sign up for gym this year. Only *you* had the deluxe banana-split with extra syrup, and you insisted on eating it all, even after you decided the banana was sort of old or the nuts rancid or something—"

"Will you shut *up?*" Debbie begged. She swallowed her

mouthful of roll with difficulty, halfway took another bite, then didn't.

"—because you couldn't bear to see it thrown away. But after you got the last spoonful down, you looked kind of green, as though maybe you'd give it back to Pete after all—"

Debbie took a quick, wild glance around, then pitched the rolls into the thick shrubbery screening the house we were passing. She frowned in distaste at her sticky hands and rubbed them viciously on a clump of grass.

"—So that was when you decided never to eat anything sweet again in your whole life," Kay finished implacably. "September 4th at about two-fifteen. So it's actually not eleven days till this afternoon."

"All right, all right!" Debbie rolled her eyes upward in exaggerated admission of defeat. "So it's eleven days. So I haven't lost a pound. So to heck with it!" She went on gloomily—"Diets won't work for me anyway; I was *born* to be plump. Look how fat Mom and Pop are—even Polly! It's hereditary. I'd probably gain weight on nothing but bread and water."

"That's possible," Kay said judiciously. "It would depend on the kind of bread. Now you take something rich like frosted raisin-nut or that Christmas fruit-bread—"

"Skip it!" implored Debbie.

The bus came trundling up to end the discussion before Kay's food analysis could send poor hungry Debbie back to look for her rolls. Though there were plenty of empty seats (we were lucky enough to board the bus near the beginning of its run), we three jammed into a double and immediately plunged into an animated buzz of conversation.

"Honestly, I must have written that stupid English theme seventeen times!" Debbie began. We all put our heads together as though she was giving us the facts on Casanova's love life. "It's perfectly foul, the number of themes that woman assigns! How are we supposed to do any other homework? It may be all right for someone like Ellen, who can dash off a theme in *minutes,* but I can't even write a note to the milkman without absolutely suffering over it!"

She stopped for breath, and Kay took over without allowing a second's lapse into silence.

"I know just the mate I want for Midge—he's a champion, took a purple ribbon at the Portland show last month. I wrote his owner right away about the stud fee. Midge has good lines; it wouldn't be fair to mate her to just *any* wirehaired. Now if I can only get hold of enough money before she comes in season again! She ought to have her first litter soon; dogs get past the safe age, you know—their bones get too firm, or something, so they won't stretch. Of course I'd have to dream up a fabulous excuse to borrow the car for a whole day—this terrier's owner lives on the coast—"

Since she showed signs of running down, I leaped promptly into the gap.

"Do you know, yesterday I got only two letters, and one was an ad? Why, a year ago I'd have been absolutely *crushed!* I remember getting as many as forty-seven letters in a single day, and not thinking it the least bit unusual. Our mailman used to say I'd get the post office upped to a higher rating, just on the volume of my mail alone. I figured out once that at the very peak I had a hundred and eighty-three pen pals, can you imagine it? And I answered every letter the very day it arrived!"

We didn't really listen to each other, of course, since we were saying nothing that hadn't been said a dozen times already. Debbie was always grousing over assignments; Kay

13

was forever dreaming about the champion puppies she'd raise; they both knew every statistic I'd ever compiled about pen pals. But our steady murmur served a purpose more vital than news exchange. In our little huddle, busy with personal chitchat, we didn't appear left out of the highjinks going on around us—just deaf and blind to it.

At almost every stop, as we neared Easton, a fresh scuffle broke out.

"No room! Gotta walk!" some late arrival was sure to bellow, straight-arming the kid clambering up the bus step behind him.

"Move back, quit blocking the door!" the bus driver would yell at him. "SIDDOWN!"

Then the howl would go up, *"Where?"* And the joker would be bounced from lap to lap till he settled on a friend who'd spare him a wedge of seat.

To sit in silence, watching this rowdydow, would have branded the three of us instantly as sideliners. And sideliners are fair game, like the straight man in a comedy skit.

"Hey, look out for that bump!" some clown might yell.

And if one of us were innocent enough to ask, "Where?" he'd roar, "On your nose, stupid!" and the feeble joke would be enough to send half the bus load into convulsions, leaving us skewered on the red-hot spit of public embarrassment.

So during our years of bus-riding (without ever coming out and actually *planning* it that way), we had developed this sure-fire knack for becoming invisible: we simply retired behind a wall of private conversation.

"What did you write about in your theme?" Debbie asked, when I had temporarily exhausted the subject of pen pals. "Can I read it?"

"Oh, it isn't much," I stalled, leafing slowly through my notebook as though I didn't know very well the theme was folded and tucked into the back pocket. Somehow it always seared my soul to have anyone read my themes. When Miss Evans read one to the class (even though she didn't say who had written it), I'd get red to my eyeballs and slink down in my seat like a worm oozing into its hole.

I mean, it makes me feel so *naked!* Writing is a terribly personal thing; it can't help but be, the way it sort of exposes a person's insides. And who wants to be turned inside out for people to gawk at?

Fortunately today I didn't get as far as the back pocket before Debbie's attention was sidetracked.

"What's that letter?" she cried, spying the edge of an envelope between the notebook pages. "Did you get another from Norris? *Already?*"

"Mmmhmm. Yesterday," I admitted, trying to sound offhand.

"Why, that's three in a week! Kay, doesn't that sound pretty serious?"

"Oh, honestly," I murmured, feeling my cheeks get warm.

Debbie said, even louder, "Look at her blush! Oh-oh, what did he say this time?"

"Nothing. Not really."

"Then let me read it!" She pounced, but I was quicker. "You see? It *is* a love letter! I knew it all the time."

"Debbie, shhh! Everybody's listening." They were, too; we were suddenly surrounded by a little ring of silence. Though nobody looked at us directly, you could almost see their ears tipping our way like radar screens picking up a signal.

But this was one time I didn't really mind. The momentary spotlight turned on me by Debbie's outcry only called attention to my exciting new status.

It's true I had never had a date; but even so, now I could *almost* say I was going steady.

Three

Norris Adair—the name alone captured my romantic imagination—came into my life last January via the U.S. mails.

Since grade school, I had been an inveterate collector of
pen pals. Most of my allowance went to buy address lists
and postage and writing paper, and the high point of my
day was easily the moment when I scooped up my portion
of the mailman's donation and scurried off to my room like
a squirrel storing nuts. Oh, the bliss of opening each envelope; slowly, carefully, savoring in advance the treasure of
who-knew-what words within!

And oh, the rich satisfaction of answering the letters! In

a way, that was even better, for when I wrote to those distant strangers, I could be anyone I chose. Elaine or Elin. Slender, mysterious, exciting. Pretty, popular, gay. Without actually telling outright fibs, just exaggerating a bit here, suppressing a bit there, I could sketch a background teeming with fascinating characters and thrilling events, leaving my own outline vague enough to allow the imaginative reader wide scope for romantic fill-ins.

The trouble was, so few correspondents responded in kind. Most pen pals turned out to be dismayingly literal compilers of dull facts. Though I always found their first letter utterly absorbing (it was like meeting a character in a brand-new book to learn that Janice Mackleby, for instance, lived on a Nebraska truck farm, was fourteen, blond, brown-eyed, rather short, the youngest of three brothers and a sister, and the winner of a 4-H prize for dressmaking), the follow-up letters too quickly declined into a pattern of "Dear Ellen: How are you? I am fine. What are you taking in school this year? I am taking . . ."

In the search for a more stimulating exchange, I bought new and still newer address lists, tried foreign pen pals, wrote hopeful letters to magazines and school papers—you know, the kind that says why you like a particular story, and then suggests you'd enjoy hearing from other readers? I worked harder on those than any English theme, trying to make them interesting enough to catch the editor's eye.

It was from such a letter, appearing in the *American Youth* Mail-Bag, that Norris Adair got my name. His was one of the deceptively look-alike envelopes I opened one January day, shivering a little in the chill of a room closed off from downstairs heat, only half hearing the sluggish slap of rain against the windows.

Norris wrote: "Your letter about 'Pick a Pretty Posy' intrigued me so much I had to look up that issue of *American Youth* and read the story again. You're right—it *is* a fantasy, but so subtle that only a very discerning reader would catch it. I wonder if you aren't a writer yourself?

"In fact, I've been doing a lot of wondering about you. I try to picture you in my mind, and have come up with so many possibilities, I'm dizzy. Your name is no help at all—Ellen Frazer; it's like a clever mask you've put on so you can watch people without being seen. And that's not fair, you know.

"Take it off and tell me about you. *Please.*"

I was simply agog. Not one of the hundreds and hundreds of pen pal letters I'd received had been remotely like this. Who was Norris Adair? And how could I possibly keep someone like that writing to me? For from the first moment that was the thought uppermost in my mind.

Norris Adair. If *he* was dizzy with curiosity, *I* was spinning in a maelstrom. Was he boy or man? Genius? Artist? Professor? He had to be young, didn't he, if he read *American Youth?* No, not necessarily. He might have picked up a copy in his dentist's waiting room . . . on a student's desk . . . in a library. He could be a writer for young people's publications, or an illustrator. Oh, it was no use; I didn't have a single sure fact to help me frame a suitable answer.

I told no one about the letter, not even Kay and Debbie. For most of a week, while I composed and tore up numberless drafts, I went around in a fog that was sometimes pink from bliss and other times morgue-gray from desperation.

"What's the *matter* with you?" Kay fussed at me in annoyance.

"Honestly, she's going deaf!" Debbie complained.

"Are you well, Ellen? One minute now, let me feel your forehead," Mother fretted over me.

I attended classes in body only; for the first time in my life I turned in a sloppy English theme that barely rated a C. I discouraged Kay and Debbie from coming home with me after school, so I could get to my desk more quickly and litter the floor with snowballs of wadded notebook paper.

At last I completed a letter that didn't seem too awful. It was very short—only a page of my best pale-gray, deckle-edged stationery; and it revealed just enough about me, I hoped, to arouse further curiosity.

Once it was mailed, I knew every word had been a terrible mistake. My spirits went plunk. Why hadn't I said this? Why hadn't I thought of that? Too late now. I calculated almost the exact hour he would receive the letter, pictured the amused grin on his smooth/handsome/bearded/ancient/ adolescent face as he read it. Maybe he'd pass it around among his friends as the latest thing in rare juvenile jokes.

The last thought plunged me into such a pit of black doom that I quarreled with Debbie, insulted Kay, burst into tears at the dinner table, and decided to devote myself to a life of Good Works.

Ten days after zero hour, the mailman hauled me back to life's sunny surface with Norris Adair's second letter.

"At the cautious rate you dole out facts," he wrote, "getting to know you may become my lifetime career instead of art. Do you suppose the postmaster will allow me a volume rate on stamps?

"Come on now—you can give out a *little* more than that. Are you a pretty young matron who sneaks away your children's magazines to enjoy like a secret vice? Are you a pert coed, majoring in creative writing (and just practicing on

20

me)? Are you a graying grandma who never really grew up? Or could you be—like me—still in high school, a thinker more than a doer, a watcher only pretending to belong to this zany human race?

"I'm waiting, madam."

Along the margins, he had drawn little cartoon faces of the persons I might be. And under his dashing signature was a caricature of himself, wearing a woefully puzzled expression. I studied the tiny sketch avidly—high forehead, long aristocratic nose, lots of thick dark hair, cleft chin in a strong jaw. A clean-cut handsome face, even in caricature, as romantic as his name. And he was young! I sighed in absolute bliss; here was a pen pal who belonged at the end of any girl's rainbow.

But my answer was still cautious. I admitted to being a junior and sixteen; I described myself briefly as "blue-eyed, dark, medium-tall"; I confided my secret ambition to be a writer and barely hinted at successes already achieved (embroidering facts only the tiniest bit). And I praised the little cartoons enthusiastically, and asked what field of art he planned to go into?

In return he told me he hoped to be an illustrator, but his parents were trying to steer him toward architecture, or something even more practical like industrial design. He had till fall to decide before college enrollment. I was terribly flattered that he had asked my advice, and I wrote warmly about the need to follow one's heart in choosing a career.

He answered that he felt much encouraged, and he urged me to apply my words to myself, too, for my letters showed true writing talent. Whatever college I chose (had I decided on one yet?), I must make creative writing my major.

State U (where Dad and both brothers had preceded me)

was my inevitable first choice of schools, I told him; and while I'd probably have to settle for a more down-to-earth major than creative writing, I certainly planned to take every course offered in the field.

GOOD (his answering letter applauded my decision)! Someday he'd be bragging that he "knew me when" and allowing biographers to photostat carefully edited portions of my letters. Would I send him a snapshot?

This was the moment I had dreaded; pen pals *always* asked for snapshots, and I took such wretched pictures that I avoided a camera like a dread disease. I stalled desperately, hoping he'd forget about it. But the exchange of letters went on—at leisurely pace, but steadily—through the graying end of a wet winter, through the impossibly bright, beautiful flowering of an Oregon spring—and he continued to repeat his request.

At last—fearing that soon he'd suspect me of being a squint-eyed, parchment-skinned ancient with a ring in my nose—I raided Mother's carefully maintained albums, garnered the few pictures of me from babyhood on that I thought bearable, cut them down to head-and-shoulder outline, and skewered them on a black velvet ribbon.

His acknowledgment sounded pleased and amused. He had taped the ribbon to his bedroom mirror, he said, and it had his mother pretty well puzzled. "Who are they?" she had asked. And he'd told her solemnly, "They are my girl."

I nearly swooned with delight. We had been writing to each other almost four months; gradually we had confided more and more particulars—the deep-down inside things— till I felt I knew him far better than anyone at Easton High, even better than Debbie and Kay. I kept the thin packet of his letters under lock and key in a miniature cedar chest with my diary, and read them all over at least once a week. But never once had I dared hope that his interest kept pace with mine, not until that letter. To tell his mother I was his girl, even jokingly like that—

By this time most of my other pen pals had dropped away, discouraged by the increasing interval between my letters. I didn't care. When I grabbed for the day's mail, it was only to look for the distinctive slanted print that was Norris Adair's handwriting.

But as yet no one knew what the sight of it did to me—the flutter it set up in my pulse, the suffocating pound-pound it started in my chest. Norris Adair was my secret. . . .

Till the day the package arrived.

Four

Debbie and Kay walked home from the bus stop with me that afternoon, their faces dark enough to shadow the May sunshine. Debbie slogged along gloomily; Kay kicked a pebble viciously ahead of her.

"Class meetings are stupid anyway," Debbie muttered. "Don't know why I let you talk me into going."

"Me!" I retorted. "What did *I* have to do with it? If *anyone* went all goggle-eyed over Ann, it was you!"

"You're losing your mind! Before I'd get roused over anything that stupid Ann Allison—"

"The whole subject is stupid," Kay interposed flatly, "so drop it."

We dropped it for the time it took to pass three houses. But our silence fairly rattled with indignant thoughts.

None of us had attended a class meeting since freshman year when we had quickly reached the glum conclusion that at Easton (as at Taft Junior High, and Walnut Grove grade school) all offices, all decisions, all honors would go to the same small group who had been running things since kindergarten, practically. So we had paid scant attention to the posted notice of a junior-class meeting, scheduled for activity period that afternoon.

Right after lunch, though, Ann Allison had cornered us outside the cafeteria.

"Oh, *there* you are!" she cried with such obvious relief we were stopped short. "I've been looking *everywhere* for you!"

Startled—and I'll admit, flattered, we waited to hear what she had to say. Neither Debbie nor Kay nor I ever spoke of Ann except in derogatory terms—like "Did you hear that dumb crack Ann Allison made in Science this morning?" or "I'd absolutely *die* before I'd throw myself at a boy the way Ann Allison does. How obvious can you get?" Yet deep down inside me (and I suspected Kay and Debbie felt the same), I followed Ann's every move with a sort of wondering, irritated envy. How did she get that way? What did she have that admitted her so easily to the charmed inner circle? A mother who knew the right strings to pull, true enough—but was that all it took?

Ann's face was flushed; her voice vibrated with emotion. "If ever I needed friends!" she cried. "I've got to make a silly little speech in class meeting, and I'm scared to death. You *know* how stupid I am—once I get on that platform, I'll probably gargle and gasp and giggle—*please* promise you'll hold me up!"

25

"H-how?" I stammered, taken completely by surprise.

"Just by *being* there! You don't *know* what a difference it will make to see friends—I can pretend I'm talking to you and forget the others are there. Oh, please say you'll come— *please!*"

"Why—why—golly, it's okay with me," I agreed haltingly, hearing Debbie make affirmative noises on one side of me and Kay mutter what might have been anything on the other.

We separated for classes then and didn't see each other again till activity hour when, sure enough, Kay and Debbie appeared, too, in the meeting room. We drifted to adjoining seats somewhat embarrassedly, making lame excuses as to why we had decided to come.

The class meeting turned out to be for election of senior officers. And the speech Ann made was the one required of any candidate for a class office—in this case, the vice-presidency.

Ann looked very excited and sort of shy, up there on the platform. Her speech wouldn't have won any honors in declamation; she talked too fast and emphasized too many words, sort of like a kid wheedling her dad for a lollipop. But even when she forgot what she'd planned to say next, and stuttered and stumbled for a moment, she made it somehow appealing. I mean, you caught yourself *wanting* her to remember. And all the time she talked, she darted those pretty, coaxing glances at one person after another in the room—

But never at us. Suddenly I had a vivid mental picture of her running around like crazy all day, rounding up juniors just as she'd rounded us up, with her little plea for help— and I was mortified, absolutely mortified. I'd been took—

that's what it added up to—and so had Debbie, and so had Kay. Suckers, all three of us.

I voted for her, though, when they passed around the slips of paper; after all, I didn't even know the other candidate except as a name in a couple of overcrowded classes. Ann won by a good margin, and was promptly surrounded by a bevy of noisy congratulators that didn't include us. We eased out of the room as soon as the meeting adjourned, and didn't say a word to each other, not a word, till the bus delivered us at our corner and Debbie brought the horrid subject to light.

Debbie didn't like being shut up by Kay, but it took her a few minutes to muster a retort. Then she said, "Well, all right, but you were just as stupid as us. She got you to the meeting, didn't she? And I'll bet you voted for her, too."

"No, I didn't," said Kay.

"You didn't?" I was really surprised. "You mean you voted for that boy?"

"I didn't vote for anybody."

"You did, too! I saw you put your slip in the box."

"It was blank. I didn't write anybody's name."

Now why hadn't I thought of that, I wondered. I hadn't had to make a choice, feeling all the while like a silly sheep being herded into a pen. I could have kept my independence by simply not voting at all. My mortification increased.

Not Debbie's, though. Her resentment over the affair had focused on Kay.

"That's just silly," she said haughtily. "It's not even democratic."

Kay snorted. "What's democratic about a class election? Talk about being railroaded!"

"All right, then you're supposed to protest," declared

27

Debbie, drawing heavily on what she remembered of eighth-grade civics. "A vote can be a protest—"

Kay made an inelegant noise. "Was that what yours was?"

"Oh, you think you're so smart! Well, *I* don't see anything smart about resigning from the human race just so you can make fun of everybody else!"

"Speech! Speech!" Kay mocked. "Why didn't *you* run for office, Debbie?"

Debbie's pink-and-white face was splotchy with angry color. She gave Kay an exasperated push that caught her off-balance. Kay lurched awkwardly, dropped a book, grabbed for it, and came up looking murderous.

I said hastily, "Mother's baked something. I swear I can smell it from here. Come on in and see what it is."

"Oh, gee, I shouldn't," Debbie protested—but longingly. Like a donkey following a carrot, she turned in at our gate. Kay sulkily brought up the rear.

Once in the kitchen, though, we forgot both argument and appetite, for stacked on the dinette table at my place was the day's offering of mail—including a big flat package addressed in that unmistakable, slanted print and plainly labeled "Photograph."

"Hey, look, what did you get?" Debbie asked in instant curiosity. Before I could snatch up the package, she was reading the return address. "Norris Adair, Benning, California—who's that?"

"Nobody," I said hastily. "Just a pen pal . . . Gosh, will you look at the size of this cake! Let's ask Mother if we can cut it."

But Debbie wasn't to be distracted, not even by thick fudge frosting curling up in luscious peaks. "Since when did your pen pals send pictures *that* size? Go ahead, open it. I'm dying to see what he looks like."

There was no help for it. Under their curious eyes I had to untie the knots and peel off the wrappings. My heart thundered in my ears as I lifted out the expensive-looking creamy folder and slowly opened it.

"Yipes!" said Debbie. Her voice was awed. "Isn't he *something?*"

He was indeed.

His forehead was almost as high, nose almost as long and aristocratic, dark hair almost as thick as in the little cartoon he'd drawn. I couldn't tell about the chin (the picture was taken semi-profile), but there was a cleft in it. His mouth looked sensitive. The dark eyes were focused dreamily on some distant spot above the photographer's shoulder.

A great surge of pride welled up in me. Not even Ann Allison could produce a photograph more perfectly perfect, more admirably suitable, than this! I hooked the creamy folder into display position and set it on the table.

"Oh, yes—Norris," I said, modestly casual. "We've been writing for ages. Ever since January."

"Why didn't you *say* anything about him?" cried Debbie.

"Oh, I don't know. . . ."

"Ellen's the secretive type," Kay drawled. "She hatches things, like eggs."

Kay was obviously still in a nasty mood, but her dagger-sharp comments couldn't penetrate my rainbow haze. Debbie, too, had become impervious. She sighed appreciatively, her bemused eyes resting on the photograph.

"Quite an egg," she murmured. "Gee!"

Five

That was how Norris Adair came out of my cedar chest, so to speak, and into the open. And that was when Debbie, and even Kay, began to treat me just the least bit differently. I mean—well, take for instance our gab-session a week or so after the picture came.

Debbie was talking about the Junior Stomp. That's the informal whing-ding that at Easton takes the place of a Junior Prom.

"You don't need a date," Debbie was saying. "From what I hear, lots of kids—boys and girls both—go stag."

"Goody, goody," drawled Kay with a dampening lack of enthusiasm.

We three were up in my room, finishing off a plate of oatmeal-raisin cookies and a pitcher of lemonade. Debbie lay stomach-down across my bed, so she could reach the refreshments on the floor. Kay was hunched up on the window seat, long arms wrapped around her knees. I sat cross-legged on a pillow with my back against the door, like the sergeant at arms at a secret meeting.

Not that there was anything secret about our get-together . . . not that anybody in this house would ever come in unannounced anyway. Sitting like that was just a leftover habit from little-kid days, I guess, when I did think someone might burst in at any moment and discover my secrets.

Debbie reached for another cookie. "I just thought it might be fun. Lots of girls dance together—"

"Who dances? Nobody in *this* room."

"Well, we could *practice*. . . ."

"For what?"

"Oh, I don't know. . . ." Debbie's voice trailed into silence. She swirled the ice cubes in the pitcher. "Anybody want more of this?"

"Go ahead, take it," I said.

For awhile there was no sound but our abstracted munching and sipping. Then Debbie said, "They go on a picnic afterward."

It was unlike Debbie to pursue a subject so stubbornly in spite of Kay's squashing. I said idly, "If you're so keen on it, why don't you go?"

"Oh, gosh, no! Not without you kids."

"Good grief," Kay snorted, "if it's a picnic you want, we can have a better one by ourselves! With a lot more to eat, too, if that's what you're thinking about."

"I wasn't!" protested Debbie. With her face flushed from hanging over the bed and her lips pouted in hurt reaction, she looked more like a doll than ever. Also like a doll about to cry.

I sighed. Lately my chief role seemed to be peacemaker. "Golly, I don't know, Debbie. It's kind of a brawl—last year didn't they have to call in a patrolman to break it up?"

"That was just a bunch of roughnecks who crashed the party—they weren't even from Easton."

"Even so . . ." I couldn't figure what Debbie was getting at. "What fun would it be, hardly knowing a soul there?"

"Well, maybe we'd *get* to know some of the—somebody."

"Oh, lord," moaned Kay, "she's been reading those magazines again! 'And there, among the whispering palms, with the orchestra weaving its soft magic spell in the background, Marcia met John, really met him, for the first time. *John,* she breathed, *all these years it's been YOU—and I didn't know. . . .'* "

"Shut up!" yelled Debbie.

It was lucky that at the moment she had a cookie, not her glass of lemonade, in her hand, because she just let fly—*wham.* The cookie clipped Kay on the ear and smashed into crumbs. I scrambled to my feet, not sure whether to duck or be a heroine and fling myself bodily between them.

But Kay didn't respond in kind. She simply got up haughtily and brushed off crumbs. "I have to be going now," she said—and did. " 'Bye, Ellen. Good-bye—Marcia."

Debbie burst into tears as the door closed with a crisp sound of finality.

I said helplessly, "Look, if you've got your heart set on the Stomp—"

"Of course I haven't!" wept Debbie. "I knew all the time we wouldn't go!"

"Then why are you crying about it?"

"I'm not! It's just—it's just that Kay doesn't understand. *Nobody* understands!"

"Understand *what?*"

Debbie fished a wad of Kleenex from my box and blew her nose. "You don't either," she said mournfully. "After all—you've got Norris."

I wasn't a complete nitwit. I not only knew what was bugging Debbie, but I became instantly aware of my own good fortune. Norris had given my little old rowboat a mighty shove. Without effort on my part I was being propelled out of the backwater and into midstream like a sleek-lined Chris-Craft. Nobody with a boy friend—even an absentee, never-seen boy friend—could be a complete washout.

"Yes," I admitted, my voice weighted with sympathy and gentle understanding of poor Debbie's plight, "yes, I have Norris."

For a few minutes—a very few minutes—I felt like a hypocrite, a double-tongued prevaricator who'd be tagged out any moment. By the following morning my sense of guilt was buried fathoms deep. Moved by some instinct that I didn't examine too closely, I wrote the first draft of a letter to Norris during social science class, covering the page quickly when Debbie leaned over to see what I was doing.

Debbie whispered loudly, "Are you writing to Norris?"

I nodded in embarrassment that I didn't have to feign.

Debbie's whisper netted me an interested glance from the girl on my other side. Casually curious, she asked, "Who's Norris?"

Red to my ears, I ducked low over my notebook and pretended not to hear. But helpful Debbie supplied the answer in a loud stage whisper. *"He's her boyfriend!"*

I knew that in all honesty I should protest—but I didn't.

He is a friend and he is a boy, I told myself. I couldn't help it if putting the two words together that way gave them a different connotation.

From that moment my status at Easton began very gradually, almost imperceptibly, to grow. I had a boy friend. If I didn't go to parties and dances, if I didn't have dates—the reason no longer must be that nobody had asked me. It could be I didn't want to go out with other boys. It could be, as Debbie was implying by the time fall term brought us back to Easton's teeming halls as seniors, that I was going steady.

"I think it's so *romantic!*" Debbie said often in open, but blissful, envy.

"*I* think it's sheer idiocy," Kay countered tartly. "She's never even seen the guy."

"What difference does *that* make? Look at all the pictures she's got!"

That was true; Norris, unlike me, wasn't camera-shy. By September, I had a wide choice of snapshots to carry in my billfold, every one almost as strikingly handsome as the photograph on my dresser. The snapshots showed him before his home, beside his car, and—the latest arrivals—against various campus backgrounds. Norris had come to a compromise with his parents—a year of architecture at a college near his home in exchange for a year at art school.

"Of course, I'm just marking time here," he wrote, "to make the family happy. Next year I'll be in Chicago or New York—perhaps even Paris. So it doesn't seem worthwhile to indulge in the usual freshman gestures, like joining a fraternity and all that. Actually, I enjoy it much more this way. Watching the parade from the curbstone gives me the whole picture, instead of just a view of my predecessor's heels; and as an extra bonus—no dust, sweat, and tears!"

A marginal sketch showed a lanky individual leaning negligently against a lamppost, while (in the opposite margin) a cloud of dust, with feet protruding below and college pennants tilting crazily above, rolled by.

"He's awfully clever, isn't he?" said Debbie wistfully. Every now and then I yielded to her pleas and showed her Norris' sketches (while carefully covering the body of the letter). "Golly. Think of you going with a *college* man."

"Next year he won't be a college man. He'll be in art school somewhere. Paris, maybe."

"Honest? Oh, Ellen, but that's so far away!"

"Not by air mail."

Debbie sighed even more deeply. This fall, she was finding me more rich in romantic promise than any magazine heroine. "I can't get over it, the way he just happened to write to you. Enough to make a person believe in fate. I mean, it's as though it was *intended*. Otherwise, look how easy you could have missed each other . . . if you hadn't written that letter to the magazine; if the editor hadn't printed it; if Norris had missed that issue, or hadn't bothered to read the Mail-Bag column. That's too many ifs for it to be just *chance;* it simply had to be planned. And you know what, Ellen?" Debbie's round doll-face was solemn in its earnestness. "That makes me feel *much* easier about the whole boy-girl business. Sometimes—well, you know—I've wondered how I—how a girl ever does meet up with the right man. I mean, they do it all the time—but *how?* It worried me, sort of. But of course, if it's fated, then it's just bound to happen."

I felt uneasy, I didn't know why. "Yes, I guess so. . . .

Where did Kay rush off to after school? She was certainly in a swizzle."

"Oh, something she had to buy for Midge. A leash, I think." Debbie couldn't be distracted that easily from the subject. Relentlessly she homed back to it. "I suppose you're just crazy to meet Norris, aren't you? In person, that is."

"Well—uh—well, of course, but there's not much chance. Look at all the kids I've written to, and only one ever turned up here. Remember that funny little blond girl from North Dakota? We'd written *reams* to each other, and there we sat without a word to say! I was so *relieved* when you happened to come over that day and . . ."

"Gee, Ellen, that was eighth grade—and a *girl*." Debbie sounded reproving. "This is *different*." She looked at me through soft, dream-filled eyes that I knew weren't seeing me at all. Not really.

This time it was I who sighed. Wasn't there any way to get Debbie off romance? And why—come to think about it—did the subject bother me so much lately? Certainly I gave it enough thought; then why this aversion to talking about it? It was something I'd have to puzzle out in the silent shelter of my room.

But when the approach of dinner hour had sped Debbie reluctantly on her way, I accomplished nothing. For I started in to read all of Norris' letters, the whole packet of them, right from the beginning. And with the first magic word I was lost.

Was there anyone else in the whole world who wrote so beautifully, so understandingly? Who knew me almost better than I knew myself? Who *was* myself—my other self? What dreams he had—and how he comprehended mine! He was the only one to whom I'd ever been able to talk with such absolute freedom about my innermost thoughts.

My scattering of doubts disappeared. The thin overlay of uneasiness that had troubled me while Debbie was here rose like morning mist and vanished in the sunshine. Call him by any name—even that silly term "boyfriend"—it made no difference. He was my true love . . . my other half . . . the missing piece who made me whole.

Dreamily I took from my desk the letter I was writing him; it was the third, or maybe the fourth, draft, but still not quite right. The opening satisfied me, but I'd have to revise the second paragraph; it didn't have quite the light provocative overtone I was trying for.

I chewed the tip of my pen thoughtfully, then got up to pace the room, saying the words aloud to get the right conversational touch, tossing in a ripple of light laughter, a delicately coquettish smile, feeling myself become for the moment gay and charming and witty and—yes—desirable.

Lost in my role, I crossed and recrossed the room, avoiding the bed and chairs automatically, not conscious of my surroundings until—lifting my head to make bright answer to the tall young phantom who walked beside me—I saw myself in the mirror, and the whole façade collapsed.

Who was I fooling? The gay smile was a silly smirk on a plain, pudgy face. There was no charm, nothing desirable, about the dull, overweight clod who stared out of the mirror at me with those pale, near-sighted, blank blue eyes. The full mouth turned down sulkily. The apple-dumpling cheeks cried "German peasant!" to the world. Oh, it wasn't fair!— why couldn't I, like the boys, have inherited Dad's sandy Scots look of lean, hard fitness? Why was I the one who had to be such a—such a *lump?*

"Ellen?" Mother called up the stairs, her voice—as always

when she spoke to me—faintly anxious and placating. "Kay is here."

I dragged my despairing gaze from the mirror. I clumped heavily across the room to open the door. In brusque ungraciousness I yelped, "Well, okay, so tell her to come up!"

Six

"No!" said Kay. "You come down."

She stood at the foot of the stairs, a flame-haired torch, burning bright. Even her freckles were pinpoints of fire against the stark whiteness of her face. In spite of myself I was forced out of contemplation of my own misery to wonder at Kay's.

"What's happened?"

"Can you get the car? Can you help me look for Midge?"

"It's almost dark—"

"I know. That's why I came. I've covered the whole neighborhood—been everywhere I could reach on foot. If

I'm going to find her before night, I'll need a car."

Her voice was so bleak, so flat with despair, that I didn't argue. "I'll ask Dad. Mother's just putting dinner on the table; I don't suppose you'd like to—"

"No," said Kay. "Hurry."

Obviously she hadn't eaten yet, nor did she show any compunction about *my* missing dinner. Where Midge was concerned, I thought, Kay could be very single-minded.

Dad and Mother were sitting down at the table—or rather, Dad was sitting, while Mother perched birdlike on the edge of her chair, ready to wing off to kitchen or sideboard at the first hint of a plate needing refilling.

"Sure, go ahead," Dad answered my request for the car. "Keys are on the television set."

"Ellen, but you haven't eaten!" Mother cried. "And here is your favorite goulash with paprika and green peppers, just the way you like it! Maybe Kay would sit for a moment with us—?"

Though I'd made the same suggestion a minute before, it annoyed me unaccountably to hear it from Mother.

"Oh, honestly, Mother, people *occasionally* have more important things to think about than food! Kay's terribly upset; she wants to find Midge, not *eat*."

"Well, then . . ." Mother's voice trailed off. She revived to say hopefully, "I'll just keep the pot warm. Maybe later will be different? When the little doggy is safe home?"

I was already halfway to the door, so I didn't answer. "Come on," I said to Kay. "Which way shall we go?"

"Away from town. She's scared of cars."

"How did she get out anyway?"

Kay's voice almost—not quite—broke under its weight of bitterness. "Mother says somebody must have left the gate open—hah! It's as good a story as any, I guess."

"What do you mean? You don't think—oh, Kay, you don't think your mother'd get rid of Midge!"

"For her it'd be easy. She hated—hates Midge."

"But why now? I mean, what did Midge *do?*"

"Nothing." Kay was silent a long, brooding moment. "I think Mother probably read my letter from Mr. Cousins. You know, the man on the coast who owns the champion terrier I wanted—want for Midge. I had it under a ton of stuff in my desk drawer, but she's got a built-in Geiger counter when it comes to finding my mail."

I felt more and more uncomfortable. "Surely she wouldn't read your letters!"

"Wouldn't she, though! Before *I* did, if she could. I should have burned it, but I had some silly notion it was like a contract—you know, so he couldn't change his mind about price or anything because there it was in his own handwriting. . . . Go slow here. I've walked her out this way. She might have remembered."

I drove close to the shoulder so the headlights would pick up any spot of white trotting along the roadside—or lying in the shallow ditch. I knew that was what Kay was looking for, dreading to see. Midge was such a jittery pup about cars; if a driver honked at her, she was as liable to leap under the wheels as off the road to safety.

The last trail of twilight disappeared. It was too dark inside the car for me to see Kay's face, but I suspected she was crying. Her voice was muffled. "Midge just came into season last week. I was planning to get the car this Saturday and take her to the coast. . . ."

I didn't know what to say besides "Oh? I didn't know you had that much money in your fund yet."

"I didn't have. But I had half of it, and I was going to ask Mr. Cousins if he wouldn't take a puppy for the balance

41

—or give me time to save it. I'm sure he would have; his letter sounded kind and interested . . . dog-people *are* kind!" she flung out, and as though the words had been the plug choking back her pain, a harsh hurting sob burst out of her.

"Kay . . . Kay, don't feel so bad!" I stretched a hand helplessly toward her, then put it back on the wheel. "We'll find her."

"No, we won't." Defeat drained all the color from Kay's voice. "We might as well turn around; she'd never have got this far."

"But she's got to be *some*place—"

"I don't think she ran away."

"Oh, Kay—"

"I called the Humane Society right away—but of course that's what Mother knew I'd do, so she wouldn't have just had them pick her up. She'd have figured out something else."

"Kay, you make her sound like a—like a— After all, she's your *mother!*"

"I hate her," said Kay in a flat, expressionless tone. "I'm never going home again."

Shocked, I drove a mile in absolute silence. Then I ventured, "There's your father—"

"Oh, him. Yes, he's okay, I guess. Or would be, if he ever stood up to Mother. But he's gone so much, he figures the house and me are her job."

I couldn't bear the sad hopelessness of her voice. But there wasn't anything, not anything, comforting to say. We had reached the outskirts of town again. I asked, "Where shall we look now?"

"Nowhere. She's gone. Mother probably gave her away. I hope it was to nice people."

I was going to cry myself, in a minute. The street lights were star-pointed blurs. I blinked and swallowed.

"You want to come home with me?"

"Yes, please. If your folks won't mind."

"Of course they won't. Mother's keeping the goulash hot for us—"

"No! Don't ask me—not yet."

She stumbled out of the car as soon as I braked in the driveway, and plunged toward the porch. I hurried to be at her side when she reached the door, so she wouldn't have to answer questions.

"Well, no luck!" I said loudly, in what I hoped were warning tones, to cover Kay's tumultuous retreat up the stairs. My bedroom door banged behind her.

"Oh, dear, dear, dear, dear," Mother murmured unhappily, looking up the stairs after Kay. "You don't think maybe just a small bowl of—"

"No, Hilda," said Dad positively. It was so strange to hear him speak like that, in such a this-bears-no-argument voice, that both Mother and I stared at him in wondering silence.

After a moment I said, "Well, *I* might as well have some. She won't want me charging in for a while. Dinner's as good an excuse as any to stay down here."

Mother bustled off in obvious relief to dish up my goulash. I debated for a minute whether to ask Dad what one did with a house guest who wasn't going home again, not ever, but decided against it. A parent's understanding could go just so far.

But I was too preoccupied to give the goulash the attention it deserved. Its delicate blending of piquant seasonings was wasted on me. All my senses were concentrated on Kay upstairs, as I mourned with her for more than the loss of a four-footed shaggy-haired friend.

Seven

It was almost ten o'clock before I tramped up the stairs—noisily enough to give warning of my approach—to find Kay humped over my dressing table, elbows planted squarely among the small scattering of jars and bottles, chin resting on her fists. If she had been crying, all visible traces were now erased. Her mouth was set in a straight, tight line; her eyes, dry and hot, were fixed on Norris' picture.

"I was trying to figure out what's wrong with him," she said abruptly, the moment I opened the door.

My tremulous, uneasy sympathy for her was instantly squashed flatter than a stepped-on bug. "What do you mean, what's wrong with him? Why should *anything* be wrong?"

"Doesn't make sense, a Romeo like that hiding behind a postage stamp. Some girl should be keeping him too busy to write any letters but the Dear-Dad-desperately-need-an-advance kind. Maybe he's dreadfully ugly—the kind of face that stops clocks and sends children screaming for their mothers; maybe he swiped someone else's picture to send—"

"Oh, sure! And a dozen or so snapshots of the same guy, while he was at it!"

"Or he's got a speech defect." Kay barreled imperturbably along her chosen path, ignoring my bristling reaction. "That's it. He *looks* gorgeous, but he stutters."

"He does *not!*"

"How do you know? Or he lisps. A lisp would drive any he-male to letters."

I stamped my foot in sputtering, childish indignation. "Quit *talking* like that! You're just trying to spoil things for me!"

"You mean you wouldn't like him if he lisped?" asked Kay, detached, analytical, a psychologist at her toiletry-accoutered desk. "Why not? He'd still have the same beautiful thoughts, wouldn't he, and write the same touching letters about them? And a lisp wouldn't change that handsome face you're so daft about—"

"I'm not—I never said—oh, you make me so mad! Of *course* I'd like him!"

"But you wouldn't introduce him to Ann Allison, would you? You'd simply crawl in a hole and die if he said, 'Nith to know you, Mith Allithon. Tho thweet of you to thpeak to uth dumb clodth.' No," Kay concluded judicially, "much better to keep him in an envelope."

If I'd had high blood pressure, I'd have been on the verge

45

of a stroke. I yelled, "Oh, why don't you go ho—"

Quickly as I stopped myself, the unfinished word hung in the charged air like the echo of a thunderclap. For angry minutes I'd forgotten the circumstances that had brought Kay here—and (I realized now with chagrin) that's exactly what she'd intended. She'd attacked Norris solely to lead me down a red-hot detour. Mortified, I finished quickly, "—go hop into a shower and dry up. I'm sick of listening to you."

"Hop into a shower and dry up," Kay repeated thoughtfully. "That's a very interesting connective. Sometimes I wonder about your writing future, Ellen; you have a certain haphazard way with words—"

"All right, *I'll* take first bath!" I yelped, plunging down the hall before I could lose my temper all over again. Bad enough to have her take Norris apart; if she started in on my writing, no amount of sympathy, however genuine, would prevent my slugging her.

As I simmered off in a stinging shower, I wondered at the ease with which she'd taken me in. What had I expected when I came upstairs—that I'd find her flung across the bed, weeping her heart out? That she'd accept my comforting hug, and be heartened by my whispered, "Be brave"? *Kay?* What a laugh! Kay had her own way of being brave; it consisted simply in thrusting out such a prickly barricade of thorns no one could get close enough to see she was hurt, let alone offer sympathy.

Dimly I realized what iron strength of will that must require. In contrast, Debbie sniffled over a mere harsh word; and while I steamed and stormed for a while, when the tears came—as they inevitably did—I'd let myself be clasped to any bosom, damply grateful for its comfort. (Of course, afterward, I was always disgusted with myself for making still another display of "soggy German sentimentality!" but no matter; next time, it would be the same thing over again.)

But Kay—

I turned off the water in time to hear the telephone ringing. At this hour? Almost nobody ever phoned us after ten o'clock. Unless there was trouble— The boys—? Hastily I wrapped a towel around me and yanked open the bathroom door.

Dad's voice, amplified by the stairwell, was reassuringly calm and unhurried. "Yes . . . yes, she's here. Upstairs right now . . . Do you want me to call her? Oh, all right, I'll be happy to. . . . Well, fine! That's great news; she'll be delighted. . . . Yes, I'll tell her right away. Good night, Mrs. Nicholson."

Mrs. Nicholson! "Dad," I cried, "what happened? Is it about Midge?"

"Yes, Midge is home and perfectly all right; will you tell Kay? Some man just called—said Midge'd been playing around their yard all afternoon, but they couldn't get close enough to read her tag . . . probably not till she was good and hungry. So Mrs. Nicholson drove over and picked her up."

"How come she phoned here?"

"Just thought it the likeliest place for Kay to be, I guess. Ask Kay if she wants a ride home, Ellen; won't take me but a minute to put on my shoes."

My bedroom door was open; I knew Kay had heard every word, but there hadn't been so much as a squeak of joy from her. I dashed down the hall and found her propped up against the pillows on my bed, manicuring a thumbnail to painstaking perfection.

"Didn't you *hear*, Kay? Midge is home—she's okay! Isn't that marvelous?"

"Yes, very," Kay said, her voice as deadpan as her face.

I wondered if the news had startled her into a state of shock. To give her time to rally, I rattled on, "Somebody just called your mother—said Midge hadn't let them get close enough to read her tag till now—"

"So that's her story," Kay interrupted tonelessly.

I was momentarily lost. "Huh? Whose story?"

"Mother's, of course. She had to cook up something, didn't she, to explain Midge's happy homecoming?"

"What on earth are you talking about?"

"Oh, Ellen, sometimes you're so *naïve!* Look, she got rid of Midge; she told that ridiculous *fable* about the gate being left open and Midge running away. When I didn't buy it, when I walked out of there and didn't come back, she knew she'd gone too far, that's all. So she simply got Midge back from wherever she'd sent her. Now I'm supposed to rush home, so overjoyed I'll forgive and forget all."

I stared at her in blank bewilderment. "You don't really *believe* that!"

"Of course. What else? After all, Dad's due home Friday. She'd have a pretty tough time explaining how she happened to lose a dog *and* a daughter while he was gone."

Now I was the one in a state of shock. I opened and shut my mouth several times before I could muster a coherent sentence. "Aren't you—don't you want to go home now?"

"Yes, I suppose I might as well." Kay took her time about replacing my manicure tools in precise order in their case. "No telling what poor Midge has had to eat today. The kind of people Mother would give her to probably think dogs thrive on tablescraps. . . . Well, thanks for everything, Ellen. See you tomorrow."

She went down the stairs without haste. I heard her tell Dad, "No, don't bother, I'll walk. It's only a few blocks."

And she'd inch over them at her own sweet pace, I thought, coming slowly out of my daze. She'd give her mother plenty of time to wonder if she was coming home after all, dog or no dog. *Why, she's hard,* I told myself incredulously, *stony hard! Her heart's got a cutting edge like an Indian arrowhead—providing she has any heart at all.*

Then I remembered her face when she'd come asking for help tonight, the harshness of the sob she hadn't been able to swallow, the flat despair in her voice when she'd told me to turn back to town. Sure, she'd like me to forget all that now; she was furious with herself for letting someone slip past her thorny defenses, even for a moment. That's why I'd been treated to this big show of unconcern—

But was it entirely an act? Or did she—could she actually believe her mother would do that to her?

Oh, poor Kay!

In our more than five years of friendship Kay had roused many emotions in me. Indignation, outrage, affection, exasperation. Respect, admiration, even a bit of envy for her super-sharp brains. But tonight, for the first time, I felt only pity.

Eight

"Want to drive to the coast with me tomorrow?" Kay asked Debbie and me the following Friday.

In the intervening days one thing had become dismayingly clear to me: Kay did believe—coldly, implacably—in her mother's involvement in the conspiracy of Midge's disappearance. I admit Mrs. Nicholson wasn't by any means my favorite character, but for her own daughter to think she'd do something like that— Well, it just made me terribly sad somehow. For both of them.

"Sure, I'll go. Love to," I said.

"Me, too," agreed Debbie. "Want me to pack a lunch?

Mom's roasting practically a side of beef today; it'll make lovely sandwiches.'

"Fine, if you want to take the trouble. I just figured on stopping at a hot-dog stand."

"Well—" Debbie deliberated, "of course we could do that, too."

Kay picked me up first the next morning. Midge, on the blanket-protected back seat, looked pert and sassy and not at all like the victim of a melodrama. She rose alertly to greet me with a frisky wag of her abbreviated tail.

"Down, Midge," Kay warned her.

Midge returned promptly to sitting position, grinning with pleasure at her own performance.

"She doesn't look serious enough to be the mother of champions," I complained. "Come to think about it, she doesn't look serious enough to be a mother. Are you sure you're doing the right thing?"

"Of course," said Kay confidently. "She'll adore puppies."

"Want to bet? I can see you now, bottle-feeding the whole litter."

"Oh, well . . ." Kay didn't appear too unhappy at the prospect. "That's a chance you have to take."

"How did you get the car anyway?"

"Easy. I just said I'd like to have it." Kay added scornfully, "Mother's dripping with sweetness and light these last few days. It's sickening."

I wondered uncomfortably how to answer that, and decided on silence which lasted till we reached Debbie's house.

As usual the house seemed ready to fly apart at the joints. How a family of only five could do this to a moderately large dwelling constantly surprised me, but that's the way it was. I collided with Debbie's sister as I went in the door and crashed violently into her young brother in the furniture-crowded front hall. This was about par for the course. I never got out of the Fuller house with less than two new bruises.

"Hi," said Polly breathlessly, "Debbie's-'n-th'-kitchen-gotta-rush-DEBBIE-HERE'S-ELLEN-g'bye-now."

"Yo," said Tom, frowning at me as he ricochetted off the settee where our impact had landed him. "Ya want Debbie? DEBBIE!"

"Oh, it's Ellen. Hello, Ellen." Mrs. Fuller approached cumbrously through the dining room with a tread that tinkled glasses on the buffet and started a faint trembling in the dishes on the plate rail. "Debbie's still making sandwiches. DEBBIE, ELLEN'S HERE!"

"TELL HER TO COME OUT!" Debbie screamed from the back of the house.

"What's all the racket about?" asked Mr. Fuller, appearing from the hall in undershirt and paint-stained trousers and flapping carpet-slippers. On his days off work Mr. Fuller spurned suits, as a woman might discard her girdle the minute she got home from town. Mr. Fuller clutched an opened newspaper in one hand and his belt with the other; Mr. Fuller's girth being what it was, his trousers had a tendency to ease downward like snow on a mountain. His family's efforts to get him into suspenders had been met with snorting contempt; suspenders, he claimed, were worn exclusively by little boys, Englishmen, and shapeless ancients ("which I'm not yet, and don't you go trying to make me!").

"Oh, it's you, Ellen," he greeted me. "Where's Debbie? DEBBIE!"

"I'm *COMING!* GOOD GRIEF!"

52

"Lazy," grumbled Mr. Fuller. "Shoulda been up hours ago, and been ready."

"Now it isn't laziness at all!" Mrs. Fuller protested. "It's her thyroid—you know very well it's her thyroid—just like it is with me. Why, when I was a girl, Ellen, you may not believe it but I was slim as a wand and forever on the go— and just look at me now!"

"Fat," muttered Mr. Fuller, turning to take his paper to whatever relatively peaceful spot he had emerged from.

"YOU'RE A FINE ONE TO TALK!" his wife shouted indignantly after him. "Look at that front on you, and every inch of it put on deliberately with fork and spoon! While heaven knows, I eat like a bird—"

"HAH!" came the answering retort like a distant explosion.

Debbie appeared from the kitchen before my eardrums collapsed under pressure of the cannonade. She carried a bulging size twenty-four grocery sack, plus a string bag of fruit. "I thought I'd better pack plenty," she explained. "You know how Kay is. When she's got her mind on something, she's liable not to stop *ever* for food. This is just sort of emergency rations."

While she garnered jacket and purse, I relieved her of the sack and almost dropped to the floor under its weight. "Oof! This kind of emergency I could go for. There must be enough here to keep us going a week. C'mon—there's Kay honking. G'bye, Mrs. Fuller."

"Now you girls be careful. Don't get to jabbering." Mrs. Fuller's voice gradually ascended in volume to allow for the increasing distance between us, *"so hard you don't watch the road. AND TRY TO BE HOME BY DARK—YOU KNOW HOW YOUR POP WORRIES!"*

53

"Yes, Mom. 'BYE NOW. 'BYE!"

The roar of the motor, as Kay involuntarily gunned it before taking off, provided a fitting obbligato to the Fuller farewells.

Midge lifted her nose and sniffed the roast-beef-scented air. Immediately she leaped to the back of the front seat, where she teetered delicately like a mountain goat, before coming to rest across Kay's shoulders.

"Get her off me!" Kay yelped. "If a patrolman catches this act, we're dead."

"He'll just think you're wearing an animal fur-piece," I consoled her.

"Sure. A fur-piece that wags. Give her something to eat— quick!"

Debbie unwrapped a sandwich and broke off a corner with which to lure Midge back to her blanket. Midge gulped the morsel without the formality of chewing and again tried to invade us. I held her off with a straight-arm jab.

"Maybe we'd better eat the sandwiches now," Debbie suggested, "at least the roast-beef ones. I'm kind of hungry anyway, aren't you?"

We finished the beef sandwiches (sparing Midge the smallest possible portions needed to keep her quiet), had an apple apiece to balance the dietetic scales, and then—after only a faint demur—accepted Debbie's offer of a peanut-butter-and-orange-marmalade follow-up. Ninety minutes from town we had reduced the gigantic lunch to the status of litter. I let out my belt two notches. "So help me, I couldn't eat another bite before Monday morning!"

"Me, neither," sighed Debbie.

"I'm practically comatose," grumbled Kay. "If I drive into a tree, think nothing of it—I'm just taking a nap."

54

"So is Midge, hallelujah. We accomplished that much."

"She'll wake up when she meets Gay Blade," Kay promised confidently. "That pup's the answer to any girl's dream."

We reached the coast soon after noon, and after only the briefest respectful pause to watch the great gray breakers roll ponderously in and shatter into coaxing curls, set off to locate Mr. Cousins' kennels.

Mr. Cousins was a lean, soft-spoken man, whose deeply tanned, age-grooved face reminded me of top-grade tooled leather. We liked him immediately; we could understand Kay's being sold on him even before he'd agreed to take a puppy as stud fee. We liked his round, bustling little wife who immediately sat us down to chicken and dumplings and milk and fruit jello. We loved the dogs, every alert and lively one of them. Altogether there was only one flaw to mar the pleasant perfection of the day. . . .

Midge would have nothing to do with Gay Blade.

She circled, she pirouetted, she flirted, she frisked; she had a marvelously good time—and (her frolicsome attitude said plainly) that's all she was having, thank you.

"I could hold her," Mr. Cousins suggested gently. "The first time a dog's bred, that's sometimes necessary."

"No," Kay said, her voice weighted with disappointment but firm, "it's got to be her choice. If she doesn't want him, then that's that."

"Well, give them a little time to get acquainted," Mr. Cousins soothed her. "The missus won't want you starting out again, anyway, without a snack."

So we went back into the warm, shining, low-ceilinged kitchen, from the windows of which we could discreetly chaperone the courtship, and had cinnamon-spiced hot chocolate with whipped cream and delicate macaroon teacakes, light as scented air . . . a sheer blend of heaven and calories.

At the end of an hour, there were only our happy, replete sighs to show for the snack—while in the run, Midge still circled and pirouetted and flirted and frisked. Sadly Kay went out to attach her leash, give the ardent Gay Blade a solacing pat, and lead his determinedly reluctant bride back to the car.

"Come on, we'd better get started," she called us from the kitchen where I was getting the teacake recipe for Mother.

"Oh, yes," Debbie agreed anxiously. "If we don't hurry, we won't have time to stop anyplace for dinner!"

Nine

'The day at the coast marked the end of our fine, dry, sunny weather. November rains closed in promptly after our arrival home, as though ringing down the curtain on the climactic scene of Kay's defiance.

After Midge's refusal to cooperate, Kay lost heart. The fight went out of her. She drooped, she dragged her feet, she sank into a deep stratum of silence from which she couldn't be roused even to squash Debbie's sentimental fancies or poke fun at my increasing absorption in Norris' letters. Though she remained attached to us (closer, really, than before), it was like having a specter in attendance at our conversational feasts, hollowly rattling its bones, contributing an occasional funereal sigh, mantling our get-togethers with a sable pall.

"Gee," Debbie said plaintively, during one of our rare moments as a twosome, "lots of times I used to want to shut her up with a sledge hammer, or something! Now here she is, quiet as the grave, and it only makes me feel—oh, I don't know—uncomfortable."

"Like at a wake," I agreed, understanding perfectly. Because it's true; no matter how much you sympathize with a mourner, it's a relief to get away from the neighborhood of his grief.

Certainly grief had no place in *my* heart this fall—not with California postmarks adding a heady fillip to the mail, two and three times a week. How could mere rain gray a day that brought me a letter from Norris? How could Kay's gloom snuff out the candles lighted inside me by his achingly beautiful, surprisingly intuitive words?

I walked through the dark, dank November days in rose-misted abstraction, recalling this phrase or that from his latest letter, or testing out answering sentences on the sounding board of my mind before committing the words to paper.

"Ellen, for goodness' *sake!*" Debbie complained sharply one morning as we three waited for the buzzer to shoo us into social science. "I've asked you *twice* what you're going to do Thanksgiving."

"Mmmm, yes," I answered, herding my thoughts like skipping lambs back to the halls of John Easton.

"Yes, *what?*"

"Why—yes, whatever you said."

"Oh, good grief, I give *up!*"

"*Now* what did I do?"

"Forget it. What's the use asking what you're going to

do when I know good and well what you're going to do?
Write letters. Write letters the whole four days probably.
Gee."

With compunction I said hastily, "No, I'm not, Debbie.
What did you want to do?"

"Oh—" She gestured vaguely toward the dripping window
at the end of a gloomy length of hall. "I was just thinking
. . . it's snowing up in the hills; maybe we could go
skiing. . . ."

"Skiing?" I was honestly perplexed. "That's a new one.
Did you get some skis?"

"N-no. But you can rent them at the lodge. . . ."

"*What* lodge?"

"Oh, for pity's sake!" Kay, so long mute I'd almost forgotten she was with us, snapped her fingers under my nose like
a hypnotist bringing his subject out of a trance. "Wake up,
Ellen! Can't you see the handwriting on the wall when it's
block-printed in letters an inch high?" She jabbed a fore-
finger at the bulletin board by which we were standing.

Bewildered, but amiably anxious to please, I studied the
notice on the board: a bus was being chartered to take a
skiing party up to Oak Lodge over Thanksgiving weekend;
if interested, sign here . . . "Well, okay, I see it. So what?"

"So the child's been into her magazines again, that's what!
Same story, December setting. Happy, tired skiers around
roaring fireplace. Tender glances. Voices lifted in song."

I heard the sizzle of Debbie's indrawn breath. To forestall
her retort, I said hurriedly, "Golly, Debbie, I didn't even
know you could ski!"

"She can't," Kay snorted, "but who cares? Much more important to know the Whiffenpoof song!" Abruptly she
stalked away from us into the classroom.

"Well, what do you know, she's talking again!" I babbled

quickly, pretending not to hear Debbie's sudden doleful sniff. "Just like old times—what a relief! Life's practically rushing back to normal."

"Yes." The word came out on a small sad hiccough. "It's normal all right—oh, I wish I were *dead!*"

"Well, for—what in—" Helplessly I watched Debbie's tumultuous retreat down the hall and into the girls' lounge. Yipes, gloom and misery everywhere! Now what was I supposed to do, go after her? Try to coax her out of there? Her social science grade was low enough without subtracting unnecessary cuts. . . .

I sighed and shrugged in baffled defeat. Even if I did follow and get the torrents stemmed, Debbie wouldn't go to class with red eyes. We'd just both end up taking cuts . . . Might as well let her cry it out, whatever it was. . . .

The buzzer rasped over my head, spurring decision. I whipped into the classroom.

The girl on my left flapped a carmine-tipped hand in limp welcome. "Hi," she said.

Last year (some remote part of my mind ticked off the fact precisely), she would have saluted me with no more than a bored glance that said, "Oh-oh, the droop's here." Last year, that "hi"—brief and lukewarm a greeting as it was —would have set me up for the entire day. But now I was too unhappily aware of the vacant seat on my right to appreciate the honor. My answering hand flap was even loppier than hers.

"Hi."

The same distant, detached portion of my mind recorded her darting, speculative glance at me. Obviously she was framing a question. I humped one shoulder to cut it off. Undeterred, she sped it across the barrier in a sibilant stage whisper. . . .

"Whassamatter? Have a fight 'th your boyfriend?"

Mr. Engel frowned in our direction. I turned even more pointedly away from her to dampen interest that once would have goose-prickled me with pleased embarrassment.

" 'Sall right," her whispered consolation carried easily two rows beyond me, "fight'th him now, that's my advice. Then you're all set to kiss'n-make-up in time for Christmas. . . ."

Mr. Engel tapped his desk. "If we can postpone the chatter, please?"

"Sure, sure," my self-appointed mentor soothed him. She opened her notebook, and under cover of a flourish of paper-rustling, hissed a final wistful commentary—"Gee, the Christmas presents I lost out on, before I got that through my head! You sure do learn fast, kid."

It was an accolade. Maybe not the knightly touch of sword on shoulder that Ann Allison's approval would have been, but a definite acknowledgment, admitting me to at least a squire's status.

And it didn't mean a thing. Across the room Kay's sharp-featured profile was again withdrawn into somber brooding; beside me, Debbie's vacant seat accused me of self-centeredness, if not outright disloyalty.

Unconsciously I let out a sigh of such heartfelt proportions that my neighbor clucked in sympathy.

"Don't take it so hard," she whispered urgently. "Way I look at it, it's easy come, easy go. Lots worse could happen than losing a boyfriend."

But lots worse *had* happened. My bedeviled conscience was already out in the hall, signing up for the ski trip.

Ten

Rolling along the highway to Oak Lodge the following Friday morning, I thought dismally that we might very well be on the school bus, bound for John Easton High.

Here we were, jammed three in a double seat just as usual, making nervous, animated conversation. Up and down the length of the bus echoed the same yelps and hoots of laughter at jokes we didn't get. There was the same shoving, pushing horseplay, quelled at intervals by the same barked commands from the driver. *"Siddown* back there, you hear me? SIDDOWN!"

Only the view from the bus windows was different. Different streets (but wrapped in the same early-morning drizzly mist), giving way to a stretch of pale-fogged four-lane highway. I looked out unhappily at wet fields and dripping fence posts, and heartily wished myself in my hide-away at home, writing to Norris.

I'd regretted my folly in signing the notice on the bulletin board even before my wavering ball-point had looped the first "l" in my name, but a sort of glum, fatalistic stubbornness had kept the pen moving. Though I knew I was going to be horribly wretched, it was something that had to be got through. I used to feel the same way on gym days, doggedly bracing myself from the moment I woke in the morning for that miserable hour of slog-footed exercise and locker-room embarrassment.

Debbie's tremulous ecstasy had been my sole reward. "Oh, *Ellen!* Oh, won't it be *exciting!*" And even that had been short-lived, snuffed out with her first anxious question, "What shall I wear? I haven't got a *thing* that's right. . . ."

Expecting a Herculean battle with Kay, I'd briefed myself with a battery of arguments to beat her down, but she had been surprisingly apathetic about the whole affair.

"Sounds pretty silly, but okay," she had agreed listlessly. "Dad's home all this week; he'll see Midge doesn't starve."

She was the only one of us with respectable ski clothes—though she didn't ski. To go with her stage-set bedroom, Kay had a wardrobe that could yield the appropriate costume for any part she might be called on to play. I had a mental picture of the caravan of boxes arriving regularly, each gift-giving date, from Portland where her Aunt Bel had some private pipeline to a swank sportswear shop . . . and as regularly, a year or so later, moving out to Salvation Army and Good Will depots. Kay would be as unconcerned about their departure as she had been uninterested in their arrival; to her, clothes were merely something one put on (1) to keep warm in winter, and (2) within the law in summer.

From Kay's plenty had come the more appropriate portions of Debbie's and my outfits. It was a pity we three were such assorted sizes, but even so, Debbie and I were able to borrow from Kay's excess of handsome Swedish-knit sweaters to top off our own very inadequate slacks.

Kay had given our attire a dubious once-over. "You'll freeze in those things. They'll soak through, the first time you fall down."

"We don't have to stay out *very* long," Debbie assured her, a-twitter with the actuality of our going, and I knew Kay had been right when she summed up Debbie's idea of a skiing weekend as a roaring fireplace fire and the Whiffen-poof song.

The four lanes dwindled to two that climbed imperceptibly but steadily; the fields gave way to trees, row on dense marching row of green, a child's garden of Christmas trees waiting for balls and shiny tinsel and an angel on top. The bus poked through a ragged fringe of mist, and abruptly we were in sunshine. I looked back at fog lapping through the valley like a gray cotton sea, and thought of a late, late movie where the spirit of a supposedly dead-and-gone character had walked ankle-deep through just such swirling, drifting, other-worldly tendrils.

In spite of myself my gloom lifted. It was good to be out from under dull dripping skies, climbing higher and higher into sunshine. When we reached the snow line, my indrawn "Ohhhh!" was as rapturous as Debbie's. Maybe, after all, this weekend wouldn't be so bad. . . .

We three were the only complete ski-amateurs on the bus.

This bit of simple arithmetic compartmented us from the moment we entered the low-ceilinged, cozily warm lodge, for everyone but us knew exactly what to do—and did it. One minute, the big room was buzzing and crackling with activity; the next, while we were still looking around to get our bearings, it was an empty hall in which our subdued words echoed like so many timid, scuttling mice.

Mrs. Harvey, the caretaker's wife, hurrying through to the kitchen, asked hospitably, "You get all fixed up with what you want?"

"Well, no. . . ." We exchanged disconcerted glances, each hoping another would speak, then all said at once, "we need skis."

"Sure thing," she assented briskly. "What length d'you use?"

Our bewildered silence supplied her with the answer. She asked, "Any of you ever skied? No? Well, don't fret—Harve'll take care of you; he's real good with beginners, and the practice slope's no steeper than a kid's sandpile. . . . HARVE!"

She turned us over to her thin, wind-weathered, benign husband whose mild manner turned out to be as fraudulent as whipped cream on a granite tart. He issued us skis, marched us to the practice slope (A kid's sandpile? It looked like Mount Everest!) and implacably, undeterredly, indomitably kept us there.

From the distance we heard happy squeals and ringing shouts. Holiday sounds. But from our soggy, bogged-down trio came only muffled grunts as we floundered to our clumsy, incredibly extended feet, only to go smacking down again with a teeth-jolting slap. I felt black-and-blue to my chin, wet to my bones, cold, miserable, *mad*. Kay looked

65

merely grim and long-suffering; Debbie, pink-nosed as a rabbit, snuffled and rubbed away tears with ice-encrusted mittens. How many hours had we been skewered on this torture wheel? I was racked and broken, all pride crushed, still following Mr. Harvey's commands only because I was too far gone to cry quits.

When at last he said heartily, "There now, that's a good start; just keep working on it, I'll check back later!" we sank immediately to the snow as though pole-axed.

"Just keep working on it!" I echoed bitterly. "Hah! After seventeen solid hours on these death traps? I'm *through!*"

Kay peeled back a length of wristlet to study her watch. "One hour," she said.

"*One* hour—you're crazy! That thing's stopped, and no wonder!"

She held it to her ear. "Still ticking."

I bent over creakily to fumble with ski straps. "Can't fool me. I've got a clock inside me that says when enough's enough."

We clumped frozen-footed to the lodge, and squatted close to the fireplace; even without song, that crackling fire was worth the price of the trip. Steam rose gently from us.

"Better get into dry duds," Mrs. Harvey warned, on one of her periodic pop-ups from the kitchen, "or you'll all catch your death."

Her words glanced off our thawing surfaces like soap bubbles. Mesmerized by the heat, we crouched before the leaping flames and felt soreness ease out of bruises and bumps and hitherto unsuspected muscles.

"I don't want to move," Debbie murmured, "ever again. Not ever, ever, ever . . ."

Outside, a triangle was whanged deafeningly, and we

heard Mrs. Harvey's voice raised in lusty shout, "Come and GET it!" Again the sudden transformation took place; the big room was jammed with laughter and jostle and loud voices, plus the mingled scents of damp wool and bubbling hot chili and fresh-baked rolls.

"Oh, golly, come *on!*" begged Debbie, somnolence forgotten. "Hurry! Aren't you *starved?*"

We ate at a long trestle table, our usual diffidence in a crowd laid aside for the moment out of sheer devouring hunger. For a good quarter of an hour there was no sound but clicking spoons and rattling dishware, interspersed with food-muffled "please-pass-th'-uffwhuffs." With second helpings came the slowdown of serving sounds, an occasional happy replete sigh, the tentative beginnings of conversation.

I was sitting between Kay and Debbie. A boy I recognized vaguely from Easton was on Kay's other side, and one I didn't know at all on Debbie's. Released from the need to make small talk myself, I eavesdropped on them.

Kay's neighbor was having hard going. "Snow's pretty good for this early," he ventured. "Better than I expected."

"Yes," said Kay, the monosyllable as unenthusiastic as her methodical spooning-up of chili.

"You ski a lot?"

"No."

Discouraged, he looked elsewhere for conversation, and I tuned in on Debbie.

Debbie's voice glowed like her frost-nipped face. "Oh, *yes!*" she was chirping, making the words a happy little cadence of bird song. "I just *love* it!"

"Been down Little Lamb?"

"N-nooo . . . not *yet* . . ."

"Neither have I. Let's give it a try after lunch."

"Okay! What *fun!*"

I gave her a warning kick—not that I knew what Little Lamb was any more than she did—but she ignored me blissfully. Debbie's rose-tinted dream was shaping up too nicely to allow the cold intrusion of practicality. I sighed in resignation and crossed my fingers for her; if her luck held, she might very well get the entire deluxe package, complete with Whiffenpoof. Stranger things had happened. . . .

From table-top up (I decided judicially) Debbie looked very pretty and quite authentic, thanks to Kay's ski sweater. But when, with the last scrap of food tucked away, she swung her legs over the bench and stood up, I thought her new skiing partner seemed the least bit taken aback. Frankly, Debbie and I have the sort of build that's caricatured in those cartoons of girls in pants; below the waist, we're just too *wide*. Nor could Debbie's damp wrinkled slacks, from which the crease had vanished, now qualify as even a reasonable facsimile of ski pants. The young man was frowning slightly as he turned to follow her out. I crossed fingers on both hands.

Kay attracted a different sort of attention when she strode abstractedly back to the main room. Kay's long leanness was perfect for sports clothes. Her bulky sweater added fullness where Nature had skipped once-over-lightly, while her flat hips and thin legs—pipestems in school dress—were like a model's in their covering of snugly fitted, smartly cut pants. Even her straight-cropped hair was somehow more right here than prettier curls and bouffants, its strange color a vivid accent against a white world. If only she'd stand up straight, if only she'd smile, if only she'd speak—

An island unto herself, she hunched down silently by the fireplace, her brooding gaze seeing who knew what in the flames. I knelt beside her. "Want to try again?"

She shrugged indifferently. "If you do."

The bright sunshine was a snare and a delusion. Outside the lodge, ice-cold wind nipped through my clammy slacks; my toes quickly became foreign adjuncts that could as well have belonged to two other people; my hands grew too numb to feel the smooth roundness of the ski poles.

Mr. Harvey, crunching past on skis, stopped to see how we were doing just as my unwieldy maple slats crossed and toppled me head-over-lumber.

He called cheerily, "That's right, keep-a-going, don't let a little spill stop you. . . . Where's the other one? She give up already?"

I flailed air and snow ignominiously, and had to be pulled at last to my feet by Kay. "She's trying another slope," I puffed, struggling pigeon-footed up the icy slant. "Little Lamb."

Mr. Harvey did a double-take, all geniality wiped from rock-carved face. "What's that you said?—Little Lamb?" he barked. "She's got no business on Little Lamb!"

He touched poles to snow and was suddenly a gaunt, weathered Mercury, darting, skimming over the frozen crust.

Kay looked after him wonderingly, "What's so bad about Little Lamb? Sounds gentle enough to me."

Eleven

The name was a gross misnomer.

When Kay and I had clomped awkwardly in Mr. Harvey's wake to the slope identified by this delusive title, we stood appalled on the brink of what looked like a fir-studded precipice. There was nothing soft and woolly and cuddly about Little Lamb; it was a steep, wicked drop-off into sheer calamity.

"She wouldn't!" Kay muttered, stiff-lipped. "Not even Debbie would be so—"

She didn't complete the sentence. I knew she'd been halted by the unwritten law that impels one to speak only good of the dead. Peering down that dismaying mountain-side, we could think of Debbie in no other condition.

The thought stifled proper appreciation of Mr. Harvey's skill as he whipped out of sight in a series of amazing zigzags, though Kay did comment distractedly, "He'd be sensational in a grass skirt."

Hours, years, eons later, he returned. With him was Debbie's erstwhile lunch neighbor, and between them they supported a limp, dangling scarecrow. Debbie, arms around their shoulders, swung pathetically inches above the snow. At first glance she appeared mashed to pulp—her straggling blond hair darkly wet, one cheek purpled with a mammoth bruise, one eye puffed and blackened. We leaned dangerously over the steep takeoff to cry, "Is she all right?"

Debbie opened the unswollen eye to give us a look of anguished appeal. My heart broke with pity for her. "*Debbie—!*"

Frantically she whispered as she was borne past us toward the lodge, "*Do* something! My pants are split!"

They were in worse condition a few minutes later, for Mrs. Harvey slit one seam from cuff to knee to expose a multi-colored ankle puffed twice its normal size. Mr. Harvey pressed the tender flesh here, there, and still again while Debbie winced and squeaked.

"Don't know as anything's broke," he said at last, "but better a doc should see it. I'll run her down."

"*I* will," his wife decreed firmly. "If I'm gone, it means no worse than late dinner. But sure as you get past that gate, some racketing young fool'll break his neck." Her severe gaze reduced us to obstreperous children who would break our bones for no better reason than to plague her.

She marched off to warm up the Lodge station wagon

while, subdued and apologetic, we packed our things.

"Don't all of you need to miss the fun," Mr. Harvey assured us. "The missus'll see your friend safely home."

But our fun—I thought the title as misleading as Little Lamb's—had been quite thoroughly tamped underground by Debbie's accident. We insisted on accompanying the victim home.

It was a grim return trip. Debbie's sniffles and occasional groans were due, I suspected, more to soreness of heart than ankle. Kay began to say, "What I can't understand's why you'd do such a fool—" and then was silent, suppressing words behind tight lips as she stared frowning out the window. I said nothing the whole endless drive, just held Debbie's hand and squeezed it from time to time. Mrs. Harvey, too, was silent, as she whipped the old car around curves with practiced efficiency, but I felt the weight of her disapproval crushing us down. It was a relief, at the doctor's office, to tell her that Dad would call for us, and so send her on her way.

Debbie's ankle was only sprained. The doctor bound it— more squeaks, more wincing—and we were delivered by Dad to our separate homes. Debbie was received as a heroine. . . .

"DEBBIE! What's *happened?* Oh, my goodness, Pa, Polly, Tom, come quick— Oh, you poor, poor little girl, didn't I *tell* you not to go up on that dreadful mountain!"

When we turned into Kay's driveway, Mr. Nicholson came out to meet us. "No trouble, I hope? No? Well, sort of thought Kay couldn't take a whole weekend away from her pup. . . ."

At home, I found Mother all a-tremble with emotion. She folded me, stiff and protesting, to her bosom. "It might have been you! Let me look at you—let me feel you . . . *Gott so danke,* you are whole."

"Now, Hilda," Dad soothed her, "you'd think she'd been under enemy fire. What's for dinner?"

"Sweet-and-sour meatballs and stuffed cabbage and date-nut torte . . . I put it on as soon as the phone call came . . . *ach, Liebchen,* don't ever do this to me again!"

"Mother, for *goodness'* sake!" I wriggled free, scowling; the Fullers hadn't carried on any worse than this, and they'd had the justification of Debbie's battered appearance. "Any mail for me?"

"On the table." I felt her stricken, mourning gaze on me as I left the room, but—good grief, I couldn't help it if she took things so hard!

Then her distress and my qualms of conscience were both forgotten. At my place at the table lay an envelope addressed in Norris' tall slanted printing. The whole sorry day slipped out of my consciousness; I caught the letter up and made for the stairs.

"Ellen!" Mother's anxious voice followed me. "Soon now, the dinner—"

"Be right down." But my answer was automatic. Safe behind the closed door of my room, I opened the envelope carefully, slowly, already savoring the words inside. . . .

"Hello, dear Ellen—all prospects point to a dull Thanksgiving here; hope yours is much more gay. The home folk are off to share a turkey with an aunt and houseful of impossible cousins—their turn on the family calendar; what mad freakishness dictates these social calendars!—so I elected to spend the holidays on campus, pleading impending exams and weighty tons of neglected written work—bushwah! I shall spend the entire four days dwelling in loving detail on

73

the most tantalizing idea born of this semester. It's quite simply this: Why don't you invite me to come see you this Christmas?"

What more the letter said was lost on me. Norris here? —in this house? To see him—

To have him see me.

The small room was bursting with rockets, popping with gunfire. Through the din I heard Mother calling, "Ellen, aren't you coming?"

"I'm not *hungry!*" I yelled. Popeyed with excitement, I stared at the calendar on my desk. Christmas. Five weeks away. Norris . . . coming here . . .

Norris.

Twelve

Debbie appeared at the bus stop Monday, balanced shakily on crutches, looking wan and pathetic and somehow noble. For the first time in our bus-riding days we didn't sit three in a seat.

"Do you mind?" Debbie asked, untangling herself clumsily from her props to drop into a seat across the aisle. "These take up such a raft of room."

The boy ahead of her looked around. "What happened to *you?*"

Debbie's pink cheeks grew pinker. "Skiing," she mumbled.

"No kidding! Didn't know you skied. Where were you?"

Just above a whisper, she murmured, "Little Lamb."

"Little Lamb! What in heck were you doing *there*—training for the Olympics? Little Lamb's a wolf!"

"I know," Debbie admitted ruefully. "I found out."

I noticed that her voice came out stronger on the last sentence, and though her cheeks were still wild-rose pink, she looked more excited than flustered. By the time we reached Easton half a dozen other bus riders had asked her about the accident. Two boys gallantly helped her off the bus when we pulled into the parking lot; another held open the school door.

"Skiing," they explained to curious bystanders. "Little Lamb, for Pete's sake!"

Tagging behind Debbie to our lockers was like following a royal entourage. Kay and I exchanged understanding grins.

"She'll get her money's worth out of that ski trip yet," said Kay.

"One way or another," I agreed.

But my thoughts didn't stay long with Debbie, any more than they had stayed with Kay on Sunday when she'd unexpectedly appeared at the house with Midge and demanded I go hiking with them.

"Midge is cooped up too much," Kay had complained. "Look at that stomach on her! She's losing her girlish figger."

"Proves she doesn't lead as hard a life as you make out," I answered absently, taking a jacket from the coat closet.

"Only because *I'm* there to look after her— What are you wearing *that* for?"

"Oh . . ." I blinked at Dad's old leather gardening jacket, and exchanged it for my own. "Didn't notice."

"You must need glasses worse than I do."

"Maybe so."

At the door we bumped into Dad, who asked, "Well, where are you off to?"

"I don't know," I said blankly. "Kay, where—"

"Hiking," Kay explained with a patient sigh. "Honestly, Mr. Frazer, don't you sometimes think Ellen's losing her mind?"

But I hadn't lost my mind, just left it behind me in my room, deep in Norris' letter. Christmas! How tremendous, how exciting, how—awful. If Norris came to visit, it could be the pinnacle of my whole life, the living, breathing embodiment of my most secret dream, or the end of everything. I was torn into pulsing, painful fragments. I hungered to see him, to hear his voice in actuality, not just in my imagination; the thought of touching him—even so fleeting and formal a touch as a handclasp—dissolved me into quivering gooseflesh. . . .

And scared me into palsy. For if I were seeing and hearing Norris, he'd be seeing and hearing *me.* My reluctant gaze was dragged toward every mirroring surface we passed; what I saw made me sick.

That pudgy, pale-eyed creature? That dumpy fraülein whose silhouette screamed to the world of plain, hearty German cooking? I looked as mentally stimulating as a slab of cold cornmeal mush. And when I opened my mouth, that's the way I sounded, too. Only in letters—or occasionally, daringly, in the vaultlike privacy of my room—could I make bright conversation. Only when I wrote could I express deep-down thoughts worthy of intelligent discussion. Face to face with Norris I'd sound just as I looked—dull.

A lump. A dud.

Oh, he mustn't come here, he *mustn't!* I'd tell him we were going away for the holidays. I'd invent a serious lingering family illness. I'd intimate, ever so regretfully, that my vacation hours were already promised too widely—parties, dances, get-togethers—you know how it is.

But I *wanted* to see him! Nobody else, anywhere, meant so powerfully much to me. Even Dad, Mother, the boys, dwindled to dim paper-doll figures in my heart beside the vigorous three-dimensional reality of Norris' image.

"It just isn't reasonable, her getting so fat," Kay grumbled.

"Who?" I asked vaguely.

"Midge, of course! Who else have I been talking about? Don't you listen at *all?*"

"Oh, sure," I said, swimming back to the surface. "Midge. Probably feed her too much."

Kay gave Midge's leash an exasperated yank that hauled the little dog back on her haunches; she looked around at Kay in reproach.

"That's just what I was *saying!*" said Kay sharply. "I feed her exactly what the vet told me to. The diet's based on her weight; she shouldn't gain an *ounce!*"

"Well . . ." I dismissed Kay's—or Midge's—problem with only a foggy idea of what it actually amounted to. "Probably she's getting too much to eat. Oh no, you said—well, she doesn't get enough exercise, that's all. You ought to take her on hikes."

"That's what we're doing! Wake up and join the party!"

There was still time, I thought, my mind barely registering Kay's irritation and not troubling to explain it. I could lose ten pounds by Christmas, maybe more; I could have my hair professionally done—come up with one of those miracle changes you see in before-and-after pictures in ads. Then with a new outfit—

"Let's go home!" I suggested eagerly, doing an abrupt about-face. "I've got a letter to write."

"You've always got a letter to write," Kay panted, reversing Midge's direction by force and running to catch up with me.

"This one's special." I was already phrasing the sentences in my mind. *Of course you must come . . . all looking forward to meeting you . . . plenty of room . . . family loves company . . . you'll make the holidays so much more happy . . . hurry, hurry, my darling, my dearest love—* WHOA! Prune out the fluttering eagerness, the naked longing. A pleasantly hospitable tone, that's what I wanted, just a hint of reserve. *What a delightful suggestion. . . . Yes, of course, you'll be welcome. . . . Mother wouldn't think it Christmas without a houseful—*and if the miracle didn't take place? If the beautician only added sausage curls to a fat moon-face . . . if the new outfit bunched at the shoulders and stuck out behind . . . *I'm so terribly sorry, Norris, all Frazers are pledged to deliver themselves body and soul at my brother Rob's home this Christmas. . . . Such a nuisance, these family turnabouts . . . I'm desolate. . . .*

It was no wonder I'd mislaid my mind and couldn't properly appreciate Debbie's small triumph as she half swung, half hobbled down the hall to her first class.

"Great snakes, what *happened* to you?"

"Oh, skiing—isn't it dreadful? But I just had to try Little Lamb."

"Little Lamb! Girl, you've got guts but absolutely *nothing* between the ears!"

"I *know*. It was such a ridiculous thing to do. . . ."

I trailed absentmindedly in her wake, glazed eyes focused on an invisible writing board. *Hi, Norris. . . . What fun!*

79

. . . Are you really serious about bypassing your family for Christmas? . . . Mother and Dad join me in saying we'd love to have you. . . . No, I didn't dare. I couldn't take the chance of losing what I had.

Debbie's trill of excited laughter penetrated the haze I walked in. I heard my name, saw that she was summoning us to come closer.

"I was just *saying*," she repeated in pleased little-girl delight, "that maybe we'd try skiing again Christmas. Don't you think it'd be *fun*, Ellen? Kay?"

Maybe my nose was a little out of joint with all the attention she was getting. Maybe the act she was putting on had begun to get under my skin. I heard myself say, loud and clear, "Well, I don't really know, Debbie. It depends on whether Norris likes to ski."

"Norris! You mean he's— Ellen, is he coming here?"

"If I invite him," I said casually. "He asked if he could come . . . I was just wondering if it would be too much of a nuisance."

"Oh, *no*, Ellen! You've *got* to invite him! Oh, how can you be so *calm* about it? I'd be so *thrilled* . . . He's Ellen's boyfriend," she explained to her attendants, "a *college* man from California, and just the *handsomest—*"

I drifted out of hearing again, conscious that the haze around me now glowed with luster tints of purple and gold and regal red. My expression (I noted in the mirror inside my locker door) was just the least bit smug. Of course I'd have to check first with Mother, but the answer was foregone; Mother simply reveled in company. *We're all so happy, Norris, that you'll join us for Christmas . . . what fun we'll have. . . .*

Because the before-and-after miracle would take place. It would, it would. It just had to.

Thirteen

Morning after morning, Debbie hobbled bravely forth on crutches to exult in the courtly little services they garnered for her. And day after day, Kay's comments grew more acrid.

"Oh, no, not *again!*" she groaned aloud when, on a bleak wet Monday morning more than two weeks after the skiing accident, Debbie valiantly swung herself down the road to join us at the bus stop. "You're sure you didn't break a leg, Debbie, not just sprain an ankle?"

"Well, I don't care, it *hurts*," Debbie pouted. "I tried walking without crutches last night, and my ankle's still *very* sensitive."

"I'll bet! Your face is simply lined with suffering. Why,

you've aged so dreadfully since Thanksgiving a stranger would take you for twelve, at least!"

"Oh, shut *up.* . . ." Debbie's scowl vanished as the bus drew alongside and the driver hopped down to help her aboard. She trilled her gratitude as fervently as though he'd spread his cloak for her to walk on. "You're all so *good* to me!"

"A-a-a-agh!" Kay muttered, stamping into the bus after them. "It's a wonder I can hold down my breakfast."

The driver piloted Debbie with fatherly solicitude to a seat. "You musta had a real bad break, kid, to still be on these things. Surprised the doc didn't put your leg in a cast. You're sure it's healing okay?"

"Oh, *yes* . . ." Debbie looked the least bit uncomfortable. "Yes, *indeed,* it's coming along just fine."

"You mean you broke it?" asked her nearest neighbor interestedly. "Gee, that's tough. I thought it was just a sprain."

"Well, it's *mostly* a sprain, but the doctor wasn't *sure—*" There was no doubt about Debbie's discomfort now; she rolled her big round blue eyes toward us in a pathetic plea for help.

Kay responded with a loud, unmistakably derisive snicker. My own answer wasn't wholly kind, either. I said, "Thought the doctor told you you'd be off crutches any day now. *Any day.* Wasn't that what he said?"

"Yes." Debbie conceded defeat in a small squashed voice. "Any day. That's what he said."

The following morning Debbie appeared without her underarm props. Though she retained an interesting limp (whenever she remembered it), a game leg obviously didn't have the heart-tug of crutches. Beyond an occasional "Sorry!"

when someone bumped into her, she netted absolutely no attention.

But she tried. She tried so hard I grew almost as exasperated as Kay. Her "Oh, *that's* all right! I'm *used* to taking tumbles!" or "Really it's *all* my fault! This stupid ankle—" were as pitifully obvious bids for sympathy as that phony limp. In disgust Kay and I walked off and let her labor along by herself.

"Sickening!" Kay grumbled. "Maybe it was her head she sprained."

"She's got a problem," I admitted morosely.

But so did I. Maybe I'd have been more sympathetic with Debbie's if my problem hadn't been so ever-present . . . right in the echoing empty hollow of my stomach.

I'd gone on a diet the moment I had Mother's okay to mail the invitation to Norris. The diet was one I'd found in one of Mother's magazines; the girl in the article had lost one hundred sixty-six pounds on it—but after one week, I'd gained two. In increasing alarm I drank my way through a week of one of those prepared liquid diets and succeeded in losing one of the pounds; but what good was that? One pound when I had to get rid of ten, at least! Time fairly raced toward Christmas. Vacation was only two weeks away, and here I was as pudgy as ever!

Then in the lounge that last Friday, I heard a couple of girls comparing crash diets. I dawdled over the lavatory, washing and rewashing my hands while I eavesdropped avidly.

"That banana stuff is old hat," one girl was saying. "You don't want that one. What everybody's trying now is steak and water. All the meat you can eat one day, and just water the next."

"Only *meat?*"

"Well, meat and greens and a little lemon juice to keep you healthy. But *nothing* else. And then the next day, just water. Shrinks your stomach, see, so the third day you don't have room for so much meat, and so on."

"Golly, I'd *die* if I had to eat like that very long!"

"That's just it, you *don't* have to. Girl I knew, she lost twelve pounds in a single week."

"No kidding!"

"Honest to godfrey."

My hands were lily-white, and my heart was high. Here was salvation. I could hardly wait to get started and watch the miracle take place.

The girl hadn't said which kind of day started the diet, so I chose the steak-and-salad and ate throughout Saturday like a camel stoking up for a desert march. It didn't bother me that the scales showed an extra two pounds next morning; a day on water only would probably erase four.

It was unfortunate that my first water day came on a Sunday. I got by without breakfast easily enough (Mother long ago gave up on breakfast and let everyone shift for himself); but midday Sunday dinner is her big production of the week. When I refused to come down for her pot-roasted chicken with wild rice, hot cranberry sauce, baked lima beans, cole slaw, and mince pie with ice cream, she was utterly stricken.

"Ellen, you're not well! Call the doctor, David—ach, I knew this would happen! All those hours shut in that cold room over her books! Have you a fever, *liebchen?*"

"*I'm just not hungry!*" I shouted down the stairs. "Good grief, is it against the law in this house if for one single day a person doesn't want to stuff herself?"

84

"But Ellen, you'll be so weak, who knows what will happen? Flu . . . brain fever . . . anemia—"

"Oh, now, Hilda, not just from missing one meal," Dad comforted her. "Come on now, I'm hungry enough to eat Ellen's share, too."

I turned my radio up so I couldn't hear the clink of silver and china. My head was swimming, my stomach rolled like an ocean tide. I lay face-down across the bed, thinking hard of how wonderful it would be to buy a size fourteen dress . . . maybe even a size twelve. Every few minutes I rolled dizzily to my feet and went down the hall for a glass of water. On a school day, I figured, this would be easier to take; there'd be lots more activity to take my mind off my stomach. As for today—well, as soon as dinner was over, I'd go downstairs and phone Kay or Debbie; maybe both. Talking to them ought to kill an hour easily. I'd even offer to do the dinner dishes all by myself—urge Mother and Dad to go for a ride—why, it would be four or five o'clock before I knew it!

And time for supper. Mother's Sunday night suppers were awfully good. Sometimes, on a chilly dark day like this, she made her special barley soup with carrots and onions and mushrooms and lots of butter and sour cream . . . the scent of it, Dad said, would bring a hungry man clear from the next town. And then of course we'd have grilled sandwiches, and whatever dessert was left over from dinner. . . .

I groaned and got another drink of water. My stomach sloshed when I walked back to my room. I sat down at the desk and began making a list of all that had to be done around here before Norris came. Parts of the house were just plain hopeless, of course; I couldn't very well do away with our huge, old-fashioned, overstuffed living-room set, or re-paper the room, or even get Mother to exchange those dreadful flowered curtains for severely formal drapes. But I could snatch up the litter of tidies on every chair and couch, and hide every scatter rug . . . truck out a ton of old magazines that Mother was always going to read "when she had a minute" (some stacks were so outdated now, the publishers had gone out of business) . . . the guest room wasn't too bad; it was the boys' old room and still had a rugged male look about it.

Meals—if Mother slipped her leash the way she did with other company, poor Norris would think he'd landed in a fighter's training camp. I'd simply have to plan menus for the length of his stay, and *beg* Mother to stick to them. She'd think the poor boy was being starved, of course, and she'd sneak in extras at every meal—but if I made the original menu Spartan enough, the end result should be a neat balance between high-society austerity and our usual wild caloric abandon.

Let's see . . . which of Mother's specialties should I include? Impossible to leave out her pepper steak—mmm, pure succulent heaven!—and her sweet-and-sour meatballs . . . and honey cake . . . and poppy-seed crunch . . . and—

I pushed away from the desk and visited the bathroom for another drink of water. The clinking and rattling had at last died away in the dining room. I went downstairs.

"Hey, why don't you two go out for a ride and leave the dishes to me? I feel a domestic mood coming on."

"Ah, *susel*, without a thing in your poor stomach? Go rest now! The dishes *I* will take care of."

I phoned Kay—she was out walking Midge. I phoned Debbie, interrupting her at dinner; Debbie described in loving detail what they were having. Hurriedly I hung up and went back upstairs to make myself study algebra with fierce concentration.

Somehow I survived the day with my dietetic resolutions unbroken. Monday I ate ravenously, limiting myself to meat and salad, but stowing away enough to keep a lumberman in log-heaving trim.

If Tuesday hadn't been another water day, maybe I'd have had more sympathy for Debbie. But on just an uneaten breakfast, I was feeling mean and ornery, and by the time I'd bypassed lunch as well, I was more snappish than Kay.

Debbie drooped more and more as the school day dragged along. The vivid color faded out of her face, and the italics from her conversation. Passively, dispiritedly, she returned at last to the pre-skiing Debbie.

"And about time," muttered Kay, whose acidity lately showed fewer signs of dilution with the milk of human kindness. "Honestly, I was getting so fed up with that girl."

I was fed up with both of them, but I managed not to say so. Good grief! Acid on one side and soggy creampuff on the other was almost more than I could take.

Especially on a water day.

I took a deep breath and thought hard about the steak I'd eat tomorrow . . . and the size fourteen (twelve?) dress I'd buy for Christmas.

Fourteen

So miserably preoccupied was I with slow starvation that for the first time in a year's correspondence I didn't count the days that must elapse before I'd get an answer from Norris. All I counted now were the hours till I could eat again.

Nor did I read and re-read his letter, when it did arrive, with my usual minute, loving analysis of every word. I only noted that he accepted the invitation. Panic spurred my wilting willpower. I checked the bathroom scales once again; my week of travail had resulted in a net loss of two-and-a-half pounds . . . and their going couldn't have hurt more if they'd been whittled off by Shylock.

Apparently Nature had provided me with too ample a personal pantry; eating all I wanted one day provided me with enough calories to coast through the next without (all my suffering to the contrary) drawing very much on stored-up fat. To get *anywhere* by Christmas required more drastic action.

I decided to take *two* water days for one of steak and salad.

"You look awful," said Kay a week later. Even in her better days, before the fracas with her mother, Kay hadn't been renowned for tact. "Are you coming down with something?"

"Quit *heckling* me!" I cried, peering into my locker mirror for proof that she was crazy. The mirror reported with aloof dispassion that she was not. Every ounce I'd lost seemed to have come from my face. My cheeks had sunk in; there were dark pouches under my eyes; my skin tone was mustard and mud.

"Who's heckling?" Kay retorted. "I made a simple statement, that's all; you look awful."

"All *right,* so I'm a hag, so forget it!" I slammed my locker door so violently it bounced immediately back and hit me in the elbow. Weak tears filled my eyes—good grief, I was *always* crying these days! I gave the door a shattering kick.

Before it could attack me again, Kay closed it with a firm quiet click. Debbie, hovering nervously nearby, irritated me almost as much with her subdued funereal air of somebody attending a particularly grief-violent mourner. She put out a gentle, timid hand.

"Don't cry, Ellen," she begged. "You don't look that bad —honest."

It was scarcely a vote of confidence. My tears spilled over, and there I stood in full view of half a hundred passing John Eastoners, bawling like a lost calf.

"I give up!" said Kay, slamming her own locker door. "If this is love, I'll take arsenic! Mop her off, Debbie, and for heaven's sake, don't let her come to class till the fountain's dry. *Gleeps!*"

She strode down the hall like an escapee from the small-pox ward; her defection made me bawl harder.

"Don't, Ellen!" Debbie begged miserably. "You look just fine—cross my heart. What are you worrying about anyway? Norris? He'll think you're pretty enough to eat. That's the way it always works out, Ellen, every story I ever read. And those writers must know *something* about it, I don't care *what* Kay says."

"No, he won't!" I sobbed, my morale too low to let me keep up a guard against her intuition. "He'll take one look and gag! I'm homely—and stupid—and *fat!*"

"Why, Ellen Frazer, you're no such thing! You're looking *awfully* thin . . . I've been noticing it lately, honest I have. Your clothes simply *hang* on you."

In spite of myself, a forlorn hope raised itself and peered out from my well of misery. "You aren't just *saying* that?"

"I certainly am not! You know what *I* think?—you need new clothes. What you're wearing fits you like—like elephant skin. No *wonder* you feel enormous!"

The battered ray of hope raised itself on tiptoe and flexed a muscle. "That could be *so*," I admitted. My tears slowed and stopped. "Debbie, let's go shopping after school! I've been saving like mad for a new outfit; maybe now's the time to get it."

"Of *course* it is!" Debbie tucked an arm in mine as we started down the hall. "Gee, Ellen, you're so lucky," she said wistfully. "I can hardly wait to see Norris. You *will* bring him over, won't you?"

"Sure," I promised hardily, my confidence starting a wobbly up-swing. "Why, I'll need you *lots,* while he's here. Just the two of us might run out of things to say."

"Oh, no, not you and Norris. But I do want to meet him." Debbie sighed in anticipation, and hugged my arm. "Oh, Ellen, I think it's just wonderful!"

But by four o'clock that afternoon, I was weeping again— it was a water day, the second in a row—and I was too muddleheaded to see the good points of any dress I tried on.

"It's no use," I sniffled. "They all look h-horrible!"

"We'll try again later," Debbie soothed me. "First day of vacation. You're just too wrought up right now. But take my word for it—you look *awfully* thin!"

Without her I'd never have survived the two-to-one dietetic death march that at last sent my weight tumbling. It was sheer joy to step on the scales that final interval before the holidays—I was forever weighing myself. Down four, seven, ten, eleven pounds!

"David, you must *do* something!" I overheard Mother beg Dad. "Ellen must see a doctor—she isn't fit for school. Is it the lungs, do you think?"

"Only the stomach," Dad assured her with insight I wouldn't have suspected. "Give her time, Hilda. Didn't you ever get a yen to be a zephyr?"

"A zephyr?" she asked anxiously.

"A sylph? A naiad?"

"No, no, none of those things." Mother gave a troubled sigh. "You're sure it's all right that she wants to be—whatever you said?"

"Perfectly all right. She'll snap out of it any day now."

Hah! That's what he thought! I was done forever with being a plump young carbon copy of Mother. Defiantly I yanked in my belt another notch and brazened through still another water day.

More than my weight was falling off before Christmas holidays gave me a reprieve. My grades were all taking a nosedive. I couldn't seem to concentrate any more (on anything but food, that is). When I studied, the words fuzzed together meaninglessly; I'd read a page and then couldn't even say what textbook I'd been holding. I sat in class glassy-eyed, torpid, my mind in hibernation. When asked a question, I blinked as though just awakened from deep sleep, and invariably answered, "Huh?"

And after it was repeated, not always too patiently, it took all my faculties to phrase a plaintive, "Uh—I don't know—was that in today's assignment?"

On water days, I tended to fall asleep sitting up; sometimes I must even have *walked* in my sleep, for I'd arrive at class or locker with no memory of how I'd got there.

Kay was too disgusted to speak to me in public. "It's too embarrassing! Who wants it known her best friend's an *idiot?*"

Only soft-hearted Debbie, sighing wistfully at this romantic proof of love's mastery, stood loyally by—and she was such a pale replica of herself, since the crutches had been put away, that her support was like being backed up by a shadow.

First day of vacation, as planned, Debbie and I went downtown to buy my new outfit.

"Red," Debbie insisted. "Men *always* go for red."

I didn't ask her how she knew. Debbie was a walking library of sentimental fact, all garnered from the printed page.

She had immense faith in fate (wasn't Norris good proof of that?) and fiction.

"And, mmm, sort of—you know—snug," she urged. "I mean, with all the weight you've lost, it's a shame not to show it off."

True, I'd lost pounds, but where had the inches gone? Off my neck—it was scrawny as a plucked chicken. Off my waist and stomach, happily—but also off my bust, unhappily. As for my hips—I looked at myself in the triple mirrors, wearing the "snug" dress of Debbie's choice, and moaned, "Quick! Help me out of it!"

With the snug dress negated, Debbie next gave her vote to one with a bare, picture-pretty top, a poured-on bodice, and an accordion-pleated skirt. "You look like a valentine!" she glowed. "Norris will just love you in it."

By this time I was past the point of rational decision. It was a water day, and I was wavering lightheadedly from two hours plus of steady shopping. I tried to clear my head and study the mirrored image with detachment. Was that really me, that gaunt, sallow girl with collarbones like the white cliffs of Dover and upper arms that—

"What's the matter with my arms?" I frowned. "The flesh sort of *hangs*. Honestly, Debbie, shouldn't I have something with long sleeves and a high neck?"

She screamed with anguish. "Do you want to look as if you'd just landed on Plymouth Rock? This is *perfect*. And anyway, you can start eating again now and sort of firm up before Norris comes. When *is* he coming?"

"I don't think he said." I tried to summon up the wording of his last letter, but the sentences had vanished as inexplicably as the pages in my textbooks. "Well, okay, I'll take it. I'm so pooped I couldn't try on another anyway."

"You poor thing!" Debbie crooned, her sympathy as warm and cuddly as an eiderdown puff. "Let's go have lunch at Pete's, shall we, and celebrate the end of that awful diet!"

The thought heartened me immensely. At Pete's I ordered everything I'd been craving these past weeks—a grilled cheese sandwich and oyster stew and a double-thick malted milk. Only when it came something funny happened to my stomach—shock, I guess. It closed into a tight ball and spurned the whole works. I kept trying to swallow, and the mouthful kept rising in my throat to choke me till I gave up and pushed the dishes over to Debbie.

"You finish them."

"But you haven't eaten *anything!* You'll *have* to start eating again before Norris comes, or you'll spoil it all! I mean, you just can't *sit* there at meals, watching him eat . . . try the soup, at *least.* That's delicate enough for a baby."

"Okay." Determinedly I spooned up the rich, creamy stew with its golden whorls of butter—and five minutes later, in the rest room that I'd just managed to reach, proved that, stomachwise, a baby was a better man than I.

Sponging off my face afterward, I peered at the green under-tint that my mustard complexion had taken on—and wept broken-heartedly.

"I look awful. . . . I don't want to see him. . . . I'm going to wire him not to come!"

"Now, now, now," soothed Debbie, patting my heaving shoulder. "You'll be all right. Maybe you just have to start with something terribly simple like warm milk—whoa, easy now!" She waited for my fluttering stomach to subside, and wisely abandoned the topic of food. "Anyway, you *can't* tell him not to come now. He's probably already on his way."

The thought brought on another internal cataclysm. When

94

Debbie at last got me home, Mother took one look and cried, "I knew it! Galloping consumption!"

She got our doctor there in less minutes than I'll bet it took him to reach the scene of a near-fatal accident. He tapped and listened and probed and questioned and then shut his bag with a sharp click like an audible exclamation mark.

"These teen-agers and their diets!" he grumbled, just barely refraining from giving the bag a kick. "If just once they'd have the sense to check with a doctor before trying to destroy their health—no, she *isn't* going into tuberculosis, Mrs. Frazer, though she certainly chose the quickest route to get there. Now, young lady, I'm giving your mother instructions on just what you're to eat, and *you eat it*—do you hear me?"

"Yes," I conceded faintly. Not for the world would I argue and stir up my currently comatose stomach. Anyway, I'd attained my objective. I'd lost enough pounds to buy a size twelve dress. Now if Norris just didn't get here before my beauty-shop appointment Monday morning, I'd be ready.

Wobbly, sick with nerves, but ready.

Fifteen

Right from the minute the hairdresser swung me around to face the mirror, Monday morning, I knew the pouf had been a mistake. It had looked so darling in the picture . . . cute and saucy with its fluff of bangs and only a wisp of hair on the sides . . . just the style for a round face.

Maybe it was the model's face, not her hairdo, that had made the picture so piquant. On me, the pouf was awful; it sat above my knotted eyebrows like a gigantic feathered hat.

"Most—uh—chic," the hairdresser assured me, but I noticed she had to grope momentarily for an adjective.

I paid glumly and wavered home, still shaky around the knees in spite of two days of force-feeding, and not at all strengthened by hours under shears and dryer. I tried to duck into the house, sight unseen, but Mother (still too concerned to be sure I'd come home on my own two feet) was hovering just inside the door.

"Ellen, what did they *do* to you?" she cried. Nobody could mistake her reaction as admiring, even though she added hastily, "It looks very nice. I am just—not used to it yet. Sit now and have a nice glass of milk and *cimmekuchen* fresh from the oven; you must be worn out."

I was, but I plodded grimly up the stairs. "Later," I called back.

"But Ellen—the doctor—"

"I *said* I'd eat later! Just a *minute!*"

Safely closeted in my room, I yanked comb and brush through my hair in mounting frenzy. It *had* to lie down— what had that woman done to it? Like an African bush-woman's pride and joy, my dark mop sprang higher with every brushstroke. I rushed to the bathroom and beat it down at last with water. Now it was a spiky helmet. Weighted with defeat, trembling with fluttery weakness, I wound a towel around my head and went downstairs to brace myself with food.

Mother, stoking me up like a fireman at the yawning furnace mouth, asked, "When does your friend come, Ellen? I must get more food in the house . . . make up the boys' room . . ."

"I don't *know!*" Why must people keep asking me? And why must the question always bring me to the verge of quivering hysterics? I drew a deep breath, and tried to say quietly, "He didn't say exactly what day. If he's driving—

and I suppose he is—he could get here any minute now."

My stomach promptly did a flip-flop; I held on to the edge of the table, willing the milk to stay down. Mother said hurriedly, "Well, now, it makes no difference. There's always plenty. I'll just put clean sheets on the bed, and run the vacuum—"

Eyes closed, I clung to the table, listening to her pattering retreat. Then slowly I relaxed, slowly opened my eyes, slowly looked around me. I had to get hold of myself. A fine thing if I took one look at Norris and rushed for the bathroom!

"It's going to be all right," I told myself aloud. "It's Norris that's coming . . . *Norris!*" If anybody knew me, Norris did.

Why wasn't there more comfort in the thought? Weakly I pushed back from the table and staggered off to help Mother.

When I could bear to look at my hair again, I set it somewhat in the old style. The hairdresser hadn't left much around the edges, but I managed a reasonable facsimile.

Kay phoned warily that evening. "Is he there yet?"

"No. I guess he's taking it kind of easy . . . driving alone like that."

"Well, I just thought maybe you'd go hiking with me tomorrow. If he still hadn't come. I'm going to take Midge out every single day of vacation; she looks like a barrel."

"Maybe her diet isn't figured right. Why don't you take her back to the vet and find out?"

"No." Kay was silent a long moment. "No, I don't want to do that. He'd just say I'd been giving her stuff between meals."

"But you *haven't*—"

"I know, but . . ." The wire was silent so long, I thought we'd been cut off. Then Kay said haltingly, "I mean, if it's a tumor or something—oh, Ellen, I just don't want to know!"

The crash of her receiver almost popped my eardrum. I hung up unhappily. Poor Kay. If she lost Midge, what did she have?

So Monday passed. And Tuesday. And Wednesday.

Thursday was Christmas. I have never known a bleaker day. Though the house reverberated with sound and confusion (Robbie and Inge came with their three pre-schoolers; Dan brought his new bride), to me its emptiness was glaring and ghastly.

Mother said, "Christmas is such a family time. He plans to come *after* the day, so he will not be in the way."

"Sure, that's it!" Dad echoed heartily. "Afraid he'll run into a bunch of visiting relatives. Would've felt the same way myself."

Friday. No Norris.

Saturday.

"I don't think he's coming." I tried to say it calmly, judicially. "Something must have happened at home."

"Of course!" What a chorus they made of the two words, rushing into relieved explanations! "Something at home! You'll see. There'll be a letter . . . or he'll be here *next* week."

The second week of vacation started. I was walking in a dream now—or was it a nightmare? No letter, no Norris. If he'd had an accident—a crash on his way here—how would I ever know? A parent didn't sit down and write to who knows what number of pen pals . . .

But I wasn't just a pen pal. I meant as much to him as he did to me—didn't I? Oh, God, where *was* he? What had happened to him?

Don't panic . . . wait . . .

How long? *How long?*

Kay and Debbie had quit phoning to ask if he'd arrived. Their tact, and Mother's and Dad's diplomatic silence almost killed me. If there had been an accident, surely I would have heard. Nothing in the papers—I'd read every word, every statistic, with frightened, don't-see-it horror—

Maybe it wasn't an accident; maybe I'd said something to offend him, to make him think I didn't really want him to come. Those horrible lightheaded weeks on the diet—who knows *what* I'd said then! I got out the letters he'd sent since Thanksgiving, realizing for the first time what a scanty handful they made. The diet again—the only significance days had to me was whether they contained food or not; the starvation days had blended into each other like a continuing nightmare during which mailtime was meaningless.

Holding the tiny packet, I felt my very soul shrivel with despair. Yes, that was it. I'd said something. . . . Maybe I could figure out what from the tone of his answer; maybe there was still time to write him and apologize and urge him to come for a *little* time, if only for the last weekend of vacation.

The letters yielded no clue. Right up to the last one I'd received, Norris spoke about coming—though he didn't exactly dwell on it, I noticed, desperately trying to read between lines, to sound each word for a double meaning, to find a hint even in his sketches of what was in his mind. Nothing . . . nothing.

I laid the packet gently back in the little cedar chest. His letters nearly filled it now. I'd had to shift my diary to a desk drawer . . . but then this year's diary was almost empty of entries anyway. Since the correspondence with Norris started, all my free writing time had gone into the careful phrasing and polishing of southbound letters; he'd been my diary, the recipient of calendar events and heart-deep musings that once had gone only into a dated volume. Oh, Norris—what had happened? Whatever it was—no matter how bad—let me hear it! I couldn't stand this not knowing any longer.

Tears rolled down my face and splattered on the slanted print of the top envelope, blurring it. I closed and locked the box quickly, trying to banish the upstarting thought that it was like a coffin. I had to do something—*I simply had to do something*. Telephone. Yes, of course, telephone—why hadn't I thought of it before? In feverish impatience I started for the door, then came up against a question mark that stopped me short. Phone where? The college? He wouldn't have stayed there for the holidays. His home? But he'd said his family was going to a relative's—

That was for Christmas, though. Surely they wouldn't have stayed for more than a long weekend. This was already Wednesday. . . .

New Year's Eve.

The tears started again, weakening me. I flung myself across the bed, letting them come, remembering the plans I'd made for New Year's Eve with Norris—

Norris, where are you? What's happened? Norris, if there's anything in this ESP business, you've got to hear me! Norris, wherever you are, LISTEN, I'm calling to you. Answer me, Norris, answer me—

The telephone rang. The shrill sound shocked me to my fingertips. I sprang off the bed, mopped my face, knowing even before Mother called my name that it was for me. Norris . . .

"Yes?" I spoke breathlessly into the instrument, my voice such a wisp of itself that I had to repeat the word. My hand was shaking too badly to hold the receiver to my ear; I propped my elbow on the telephone table. "Yes?"

Sixteen

"Is that you, Ellen?"

It was Mrs. Fuller. The strength flowed out of me like water. A spent bow, I leaned over the table, feeling vitality drain away. Such defeat engulfed me that I willed myself to lose consciousness, to drift out of reach of sound, to die. Stubbornly my senses continued to function, even to register Mrs. Fuller's message.

"I was just wondering if you'd like to come over this evening, Ellen, you and Kay. Maybe spend the night?" Her voice was unusually subdued, almost cautious, as though between words she darted glances over her shoulder to be sure she wasn't overheard.

I clung to the cold metal of the phone, dredging up words to fill the vacuum left by her questioning silence. "Well . . . I don't know . . . Mrs. Fuller. I'm . . . sort of . . . busy . . ." My brain labored slowly into renewed action. Think of something, think of something (I begged it)— don't make me take a dead and buried heart to that loud-with-life house. . . .

Mrs. Fuller's voice, still unnaturally low, but rapid and urgent, cut across my fumbling excuses. "I'll tell you how it is, Ellen. Debbie isn't feeling so well, and I hate to go out this evening and leave her alone. But we've been promised to this party for weeks, and it's bridge—you know how upsetting it is for a hostess, a couple dropping out at the last minute—"

I was swept over the waterfall of her words, bruised black and blue by their sound, drowned in their noisy excess.

"—Of course Tom'll be here, but what good's a little boy when a person's feeling lowdown and miserable, acting like she might die any minute—"

Common decency forced me to ask, "What's wrong with her?" though so numb was I inside that I didn't really care.

"Well, she took a tumble—I *told* her not to climb that rickety bunch of boxes, but she *would* try to reach the top shelf in her closet, looking for an evening bag she'd got once as a gift and never used—'Just the thing for Polly to carry,' she said, though Polly said, 'Don't bother'—and of course, wouldn't you know it, the boxes went every which way and poor Debbie with them."

"Polly?" I repeated vaguely, not at all sure I was hearing right. "Evening bag?"

"Yes, to take to the dance. Though it's really not *that*

103

formal, just a New Year's Eve party—but you know how children are these days, everything has to be done like grown-ups, dates and long dresses and a corsage from the florist, if you can believe it! I told Pa, just because we started out with a nice sensible daughter like Debbie doesn't mean we'll be lucky twice. Polly's another kettle of fish entirely, I said; we'll have our hands full with that one. But anyway, here's poor Debbie taken to her bed, and everybody off to celebrate the New Year, it doesn't seem fair—"

"What did she break?" I asked, hearing my polite show of concern and wondering at the natural way a body and mind could function after all sensation had been cut off.

"Nothing, nothing at all—she was positive she'd cracked a rib, but we had the doctor right away and he said only bruises. But the way she carried on, you'd think he'd ordered her into a cast—burst into tears, and been crying ever since— won't get out of her bed. I do hope he knew what he was talking about; there's such a thing as internal injuries—oh, dear, maybe Pa and I *shouldn't*—"

"I'll come over," I promised, making an almost physical effort to shake off the lethargy weighing me down. "You leave a number where I can reach you—just in case."

"Oh, thank you, Ellen! I'll feel so much better. . . . Maybe you girls could have a little New Year's party of your own, you always have such a good time together, not needing boys around, like some girls do. . . . Tell you what, I'll make sandwiches and fruit punch before I go, and you can help yourself to ice cream from the freezer . . ."

"Thank you, Mrs. Fuller," I remembered to say politely before hanging up, then a moment afterward wondered if I'd cut her off in mid-sentence. Well, no matter. Still functioning on automatic drive, a dutiful, well-trained robot, I dialed Kay's number and relayed Mrs. Fuller's invitation.

Kay's voice was muffled. "Oh, I don't know," she began, not troubling to invent an excuse, "I don't really want to go."

"Neither do I," I admitted. "But I guess I'll have to, now I've promised. Why don't you come, too? The more there are, the less dismal it'll be."

"I don't want to leave Midge. She's acting—odd. Sort of restless, and panting. Won't eat." Kay's voice was almost inaudible.

I didn't know what to say. I knew she was suffering, and yet the fact touched only the shallows of my mind; I had no help to offer, so at last, saying nothing, I hung up. My robot was running down; I'd exhausted my stock of automatically polite phrases on Mrs. Fuller and now must wait to be rewound.

Mother was hovering just within earshot in the kitchen. She asked anxiously, "There is trouble at the Fullers'?"

"Nothing too serious. Debbie took a header, but she's only bruised."

"Ah, the poor girl! Another fall, so soon again! Maybe you could take her some of my cherry torte? Or perhaps—"

The familiar offer . . . Mother's remedy for any ill. What would she bake for a broken heart? It would have to be something exquisitely light—

"Almond horns?" Startled, I realized she was still talking about Debbie. "She is very fond of them, and it wouldn't take me any time at all . . ."

How puckered her face was! I was so used to its apple roundness that I hadn't noticed the new lines anxiety had added. *She's been worrying about me* (it was the first thought to dip below the smooth shell of my mind instead of skidding right off); *she's been all torn up this past week, grieving right along with me, and not saying a word except with her hands.* Her clever, loving, *giving* hands.

The shell broke wide open; my numbness was burst and scattered and driven before the violent hurting upheaval of awakened sensation. "Mommy . . ." I hadn't called her that since pre-school days. Why did the name come back to me now? "Mommy . . ." and I was hugging her so hard I felt the breath go out of her, both of us crying and trying to cover it with laughter. "Yes, almond horns—they'd make *anyone* feel better—*nobody* makes almond horns like yours! What can I do to help?"

"Ach, just go make yourself pretty—the new dress maybe? Such a cheerful color, it will surely brighten her spirits to see you."

The new dress, bought for Norris, never put on since the day at the store. "Much too dressed up," I said hurriedly. "But I'll wear the red wool—how'll that be?—and lots of glitter. Debbie hasn't seen my new necklace . . . it'll dazzle her blind . . . with lots of bracelets . . ."

That was the solution. Talk fast, move fast, keep one jump ahead of the hurt till it was bearable . . . if it was ever bearable . . .

I was covering the plate of pastry with wax paper that evening, when a horn beeped in the driveway and I went out to find Kay at the wheel of her mother's car. "Ready?" she asked, staring straight ahead, her thin freckled face carefully expressionless.

"Sure, just a minute." I wanted to ask what had changed her mind, but didn't. Kay gave explanations only in her own good time.

Balancing Mother's heaped offering with care, I slid in

beside her. "Nice you could get the car; these'd be tricky to carry."

She maneuvered out of the driveway and turned toward Fullers'. "Dad's out of town, so Mother wasn't going anywhere tonight. . . . Anyway, I had an errand downtown first." We covered two blocks in silence before she added, "I took Midge to the animal hospital."

"Oh, Kay, is she worse?"

"No." The single, carefully shaped word held me off like a stiff, straight arm. "I just figured it wasn't fair to her, that's all. Pretending nothing was wrong."

"What did the vet say?"

"He wasn't there yet. Only a stupid boy. I wrote down Debbie's number so he could call me as soon as he came in. The boy acted as though *I* was the idiot—grinning and gibbering 'Won't happen *that* fast!'—but I guess he has wits enough to deliver a message."

I sought for something reassuring that I could say without being labeled "idiot" in turn. "I wish I knew more about dogs."

"So do I. I never had a pet before. Not even a guinea pig. Not even a canary. Dirty, all of them—scattering seeds and chewing up rugs and making messes—" Now her words came in harsh, tearing spurts. "I shouldn't have let them give me Midge. They'd have found somebody else, somebody who was used to animals, who knew what to do for them . . ."

"Kay, quit knocking yourself! You did the best you could."

"No, I didn't. I should have taken her to the vet two weeks ago—I even kept her out of Dad's sight, when he was home last time, scared he'd say, 'What's wrong with her?' What if I waited too long?"

It was a relief to see the Fuller house, ablaze with lights, rocketing with noise. Tom let us in. The television volume was turned high; a radio blasted in competition. Tom shouted, "Everybody's upstairs! You want me to call 'em?"

"No, we'll go on up, if it's okay."

"Sure!" He plunged for the living room from which he'd emerged to act as host. I ducked just in time. From the doorway, he yelled, "Pretty soon it's gonna be New Year's in New York! You want me to tell you when?"

"That'll be swell," I conceded.

"I'm gonna see New Year's in clear across the country! I get to stay up till it's New Year's here!"

"Goody," said Kay.

On the stairs, we had a near miss with Polly, who rushed down, exclaiming, "Oh, it's *you!* I thought it was—" and then, over the sustained peal of the doorbell, *"There* he is!"

I looked after her in bewildered disbelief. "That *was* Polly, wasn't it?" Ballerina-length red taffeta, long white gloves, blond hair scooped high above baby face and ringed with a circlet of rosebuds.

Kay said, "Poor Debbie."

A second surge flattened us against the wall. Mrs. Fuller, a talcum-scented tidal wave, exhaled in loud relief. "You're here! I feel *so* much better. Just go right on up—I've been tidying the mess Polly left, so the room would be nice for visiting. If you can get Debbie to eat—she wouldn't touch but a bite of supper, but I left plenty for all of you in the oven—I'M *COMING,* PA!—mark my words, that man'll have a stroke someday, bellowing like that!"

After the uproar of their departure, the hall seemed deathly quiet. We tiptoed down its length to peer uneasily into Debbie's room. Flat on the bed, gently shadowed by the subdued light, she raised two fingers in a limp gesture of welcome.

"Hi. Nice of you to come. I suppose Mom told you what happened?"

She looked terrible, almost worse than when they'd carried her up Little Lamb. Her face was puffed, her eyes diminished to slits, her skin a sort of raw red. It was hard to imagine Debbie weeping like that—easy sentimental tears, yes, but not such a frightening storm.

"What an *awful* shame," I murmured in pity. "Are you feeling any better yet?"

She made a faint, testing movement, winced and smiled bravely. "N-not *really*."

"Mother sent some almond horns." I set the dish on the table beside her. "She baked them specially for you, soon as she heard the news. You know Mother—all her cures come from cookbooks."

"She's a dear. They do look lovely, but I don't believe— well, maybe just a *piece* of one . . ."

Kay made an indeterminate noise, the first sound I'd heard from her since we entered the room. Now she pulled a chair forward noisily, shattering the invalid-quiet, and turned on a bright overhead light. "D'you mind? Can't see whether I'm eating pastry or my fingers, otherwise. You *were* going to offer me some, weren't you?"

"Oh, *yes!*" Debbie apologized. In the heightened glare her grief-swollen face was exposed like an open wound; I could have murdered Kay for turning the light on. "Do help yourself. I'm afraid I can't quite reach—"

I hurried to take over serving duties, then hovered solicitously over the bed, wondering what I could do for her comfort. "Could you sit up, Debbie, if I got more pillows?"

"I could *try*."

Kay didn't offer any assistance as I boosted Debbie's limp weight forward, and gently padded the space with pillows. I frowned at her from behind Debbie's shoulder. Ignoring me elaborately, she helped herself to another almond horn.

"You two had better eat fast, or I'll have these all gone." Casually she kicked off her flats, tilted back in her chair and put her feet up on Debbie's bed with a thumping whack. Debbie shuddered faintly; my own nerves felt a sympathetic twinge. I was beginning to wish heartily I hadn't urged Kay to come.

"Go right ahead," Debbie told her, looking carefully away from the dwindling supply of pastry. "I'm scarcely eating a *thing* yet. . . ."

"Why not? Didn't hurt your stomach, did you?"

Debbie's soft childlike mouth quivered. "I guess *you* wouldn't feel like eating, either, if you'd practically smashed yourself flat—"

"Oh, that. Just a few bruises, didn't your mother say?"

I glared at Kay in mounting indignation. Debbie's breath caught on a little sob. Any minute now, Kay would have her crying again—*darn* Kay!—what had got into her?

From the foot of the stairs, Tom roared, *"Kay! Telephone!"*

Kay's face closed like a book snapped shut. She was out of the chair and the room before the echo of Tom's voice had died away. I looked helplessly at her left-behind flats— scuffed, broken across the toes, immensely long (how Kay hated her big feet!)—and didn't know which of us to feel sorriest for.

Debbie sniffled plaintively. I said, "Look, don't let her upset you—you know how Kay talks."

"She s-sounds as if—as if it's *fun,* getting b-bunged up!"

"She doesn't mean to, Debbie. Trouble is, tonight she's all wrought up herself. She took Midge to the animal hospital on her way here."

"All she c-cares about is that d-dog! Midge means more to her than *anybody*—"

"Oh, no, Debbie—"

"Even her own f-family! You *know* it's so! We're just n-nothing—"

Kay's yell put to shame any roar yet heard under the Fuller roof. She came whooping up the stairs, two and three at a time. Her face blazed like a thousand-watt bulb.

"You know what's wrong with Midge? *D'you know what's wrong with Midge!* She's going to have *puppies!* Any day now. PUPPIES!"

"But—but *how*—" I goggled.

Debbie, still resentful, said, "You mean you couldn't tell? Why, even *Tom* would know if a dog's going to have pups—"

"The vet said lots of people get fooled on a first litter; sometimes a dog doesn't show any signs of it till the last couple of weeks."

"I still don't see—" I began.

Debbie relentlessly pursued her momentary advantage. "Even so, you must be pretty stupid not to know—"

Kay turned full wattage on the grumbling recumbent figure, one long finger pointed dead-level at Debbie like an unsheathed sword. "No more stupid than you, Debbie Fuller! Trying to put yourself back on crutches because you're jealous of Polly!"

In the abrupt silence that fell like a paralysis on the room, I heard my own quick indrawn breath. Of course.

Kay was right. If my wits had been working in even low gear when Mrs. Fuller phoned, I'd have known it myself.

Then Debbie, all the fight gone out of her, was whimpering, "I didn't—I'm not—I don't know what you're talking about!"

"Oh, yes, you do," Kay overrode the whimper calmly. "And it was a pretty ridiculous thing to do, if you ask me. So you went headfirst down Little Lamb and got treated like a hero for a while—did you think falling off a chair would give you a repeat performance?"

"It w-wasn't a chair—"

"No, of course not. A chair would've been too steady. That's why the boxes."

Debbie began to sob loudly. My heart twisted with pity for her. "Stop it!" I ordered Kay angrily. "Shut *up!*"

"I certainly won't. There's been entirely too much shutting up. Be tactful, pretend you don't notice, *shut up*—and let Debbie break her neck, next try—is that what you want? That'd get her plenty of attention all right—John Easton turning out for the funeral in a body—everybody snuffling 'so sad, so young!' But what if she only put herself permanently into a wheelchair? People get sick of trotting around with flowers and candy after awhile, but the poor stupe'd still have to live out her life, with or without sympathetic visitors . . ."

"All *right!*" I yelled at her. "So what's all your talk going to do for Debbie except make her feel worse?"

"Keep her from doing it again," Kay said, unperturbed by our reaction. "That's kind of negative, I admit, but it's a start. You can't solve a problem till you admit it's there."

In spite of myself, my attention was snagged. I noticed that Debbie, too, was sobbing on a lower key that didn't

112

interfere with her hearing. Kay tilted back again in her chair, propped her feet on the bed, and reached for another almond horn.

"If having a date means that much to Debbie," she announced serenely, "we'll have to get her one. Maybe it's high time we all got started. Not that I care personally," she added quickly, "but even *I* would prefer to be a spinster by choice, not necessity. Way things are going now, we three are riding straight for the biggest batch of nasty complexes ever hatched at John Easton."

"The Unchosen," I murmured—and instantly regretted saying it aloud as I met the battery of their brooding glances.

"Good name," Kay agreed after a pause.

"But not for you." Debbie sniffled. "You've got Norris."

"Norris?" What immense effort it took to repeat the name lightly, carelessly! "Who's he? How do I know there *is* a Norris? Scratch Norris." The words made intelligible sound, but what they did to my heart was chaotic. I lifted my chin and made myself meet Kay's and Debbie's stares without flinching.

"Attagirl," said Kay. "So we're a team. Are you both game to figure out what we can do, or do you want to go on pretending it isn't so?"

"Up and at 'em, cap," I assured her. "I'm right behind you."

Debbie looked ready to cry again.

"Well, *are* you with us or aren't you?" Kay demanded.

"I—I guess so."

"All right then. It's really very simple—just a matter of applying mathematical principles. Let's get to work on a plan right now—okay?"

"Not yet," I demurred. "First I want to know, how come

Midge is having puppies? Gay Blade never got close—"

"Oh, they'll be crossbreeds, of course," Kay said with cheerful acceptance. "A love match."

"A love match *when?* Midge never got outside her run except—except that day—"

Kay's face sobered into sudden thoughtfulness. "Yes," she said, "that's right, isn't it? Except that day—"

"When somebody left the gate open and she ran away." I stressed each word firmly. "Just like your mother said."

"Yes," Kay repeated, her voice oddly far away. The candle-power was turned on in her face again, but now it burned on a gentler wattage. "Yes, just like she said."

"*Hey!*" Tom yelled up the stairs. "Hey, you guys, *listen*— it's happy New Year in New York!"

"It's happy New Year right here!" I shouted back at him. Kay grinned at me lopsidedly; Debbie joined in with a watery little smile.

"Should auld acquaintance be forgot—" Kay launched the song valiantly, offkey in her unsteady soprano. Debbie and I lent our support.

Norris, my heart beat out the syllables beneath the music's rhythm, *Norris, where are you?—what happened—how long will it hurt like this?—Norris, oh, Norris . . .*

Seventeen

Loren Marsh (B).
Stuart Schofield (S).
Roger Austen (SB; P).
Max Wilson (S; P?).
Bill Whitaker (B; S).

"Who else?" Kay tapped her pencil imperatively. "Ought to be lots more. Think!"

"We-ell . . ." Debbie twisted her brows in anguished effort to place the nameless, almost faceless horde of trousered figures in Easton's huge classes. "There's Bob Endicott—"

"Nope. Definitely the Ann Allison type."

"That's what you say about practically everybody I name!"

"Because that's practically all the names you know. No wonder you never get yourself a date. You sit there in class and goggle at the big wheels, instead of going after the little spokes!"

The list was the first step in Kay's application of mathematical principles.

"Out of a given number of unattached boys," she pronounced authoritatively, stabbing the air from time to time with her pencil like a torero making passes at an unseen bull, "you've got to figure that a certain percentage will react with mild interest to the right approach. Of that number, a smaller segment will show positive interest, and out of that group, a tiny nucleus should prove ultimately available. D'you follow?"

"No," I said. Debbie shook her head in bewilderment.

Kay gave an exasperated sigh. On occasion, our second-rate mental capacity (especially in mathematics) was a trial to her. "Look, it all boils down to having enough names to start with. Like rallying voters, or passing out samples of a new product—*everybody* won't vote for your candidate, and *everybody* won't rush out and buy your product, but a certain percentage will. So the more people you canvass, the bigger your percentile of success. It's a fundamental law—like gravity, or centrifugal force."

Debbie looked at me helplessly. "Does it make sense to *you?* I'm kind of lost."

"Oh, good grief, it's as simple as two plus two!" Kay said impatiently. "If you want to end up with five boys, and you're only netting ten percent, you'd have to start out with fifty—see?"

"Gee," murmured Debbie, the blissful thought of five boys erasing her doubts as to how Kay proposed to snare them. "Well, okay, how about that kid with big glasses and kind of long hair in English lit—you know, the one who answers the questions nobody else knows? What's his name—Bernard something—Bernard Keller?"

Bernard Keller, Kay added the name to our list, and put after it the letter (B).

B for brain. SB for semi-brain. S for shy. P for poor. PP for dead-broke. These were our code letters, with a sprinkling of question marks when we disagreed.

"Lots of boys at Easton don't date," Kay had stated firmly in her opening lecture. "They're too busy studying, or they're scared of girls, or they figure they can't afford it or haven't a car or the right clothes. *They* won't ask a girl for a date, so it's up to us to search them out and make the first proposal."

"Huh? Oh, golly, *wait* a minute!" Debbie protested.

"Not me," I joined her. "If that's your plan, count me out."

Kay looked ready to give us both up and retire to permanent single-blessedness.

"Oh, you morons, of *course* I don't mean walk up to a boy and say, 'Hey, how about taking me to the show tonight?' You've got to be *subtle.* You've got to plan your tactics, like a general before the battle. What we're going to do is surround and infiltrate, but so quietly they won't even know they've been conquered." She looked at our blank faces, and flung out her arms in despair. "Look, just help me make up this list, and I'll brief you as we go along—okay?"

"But I don't want to. It sounds so—so—"

"Calculating," I helped Debbie out.

"You want dates, don't you?" Kay asked. "Do you know any better way to get them?"

"I don't know *any* way," Debbie confessed forlornly. "You know I don't. But I thought—"

"You thought you could just sit tight and true love would come along, like in the movies. Well, it won't. You've got to go out and get it."

"Ann Allison doesn't—"

"Oh, come off it! She's working at it every minute, and so are all the other girls in that crowd, and so are their mothers! Maybe they don't spell it out, the way we're doing, but they're out to get their man as sure as any two-gun, tall-in-the-saddle, horse-opera hero!"

"How do *you* know so much about it?" Debbie was getting nettled, as she always did, at Kay's don't-argue-with-me declarations.

"Because I keep my eyes and ears open, that's how." Kay jabbed the air and brought the bull to its knees. "Because my mind isn't a glue pot of romantic nonsense. Because I see things as they are."

"Like you did with Midge?" It was too good an opening; I couldn't resist inserting a dart of my own.

Kay's face colored with joyous warmth, and her eyes looked more star-filled than Debbie's at her dreamiest. Midge had been safely delivered of four wriggling mouse-sized puppies on New Year's Day—their appearance putting the finger of fatherhood indisputably on a beagle in the next block—and Kay had been riding a rainbow ever since.

We had both been summoned to her home Friday to help her enlarge Midge's run and doghouse in preparation for the new family's arrival home.

"Let's see now, we have to offset the entrance so there

won't be a draft—mmm, easiest way would be to put a box across the opening, with holes cut out here and here—make the house L-shape, huh? You two drive in more stakes for the fence. . . ."

From time to time, Mrs. Nicholson appeared apprehensively on the back porch to red-pencil our labors. "No, no, girls, not so close to my rhododendron!" she cried. And another time, "Oh, dear, *must* you fence in the barberry bush? The dogs will ruin it!" And a final plaintive complaint, "Kay, why do you need so much of the yard? The puppies won't be here *that* long!"

"Where will they be?" Kay demanded, cheerfully pounding and hauling and growing dirtier and happier by the minute.

"Why, I thought—well, there's the animal shelter. After all, they *are* just mongrels—"

Kay laid down her hammer with ominous gentleness. "Crossbreeds," she corrected. "Pure-bred parents of different breeds do *not* have mongrels."

"Even so, all I meant was—"

"Most of our present canine strains were crossbreeds to begin with." Kay was already beginning to talk like a dog encyclopedia. She had brought home all the free booklets provided by the vet, and collected another armful of volumes from the library. "A crossbreed is very often healthier and smarter than a dog that has been too finely bred."

"What I was trying to say was—"

"So naturally we have to give them time to show their good points before we can find the right homes for them," Kay went raptly on, astride her rainbow and galloping high. "I imagine it'll take months!"

"Months," Mrs. Nicholson echoed faintly. "Oh, dear."

But obviously distraught though she was, I thought Mrs. Nicholson was accepting the upheaval of her backyard landscaping surprisingly well. From relief, maybe, at having Kay put off the steely suit of armor she'd worn since Midge's brief exodus? True, Kay was prickly as ever, but who wouldn't rather cope with a tart-tongued thistle than a battery of deadly silent bayonets?

For a week now the puppies had provided the high point of Kay's days, their care a matter of greater moment than her straight-A average. To listen to her, you'd think she'd never once spoken of raising champion wire-haireds. Why, no pedigreed pooch had an iota of distinction that couldn't be bettered by Midge's litter! The puppies' remarkable health, appetite, cleverness, strength, ingenuity filled her conversation.

"If they're such a good cross, maybe you've got a new breed," I suggested, going along solemnly with her enthusiasm. "Why don't you give them a name? Bea-ters. No, that's not so good. How about Ter-gles?"

"The Terrible Tergles," Debbie giggled.

" 'Tergles,' " I quoted an as yet unwritten encyclopedia, " 'first appeared in the northwestern part of the United States about the middle of the twentieth century. It is not known exactly how the strain originated, but it is believed that an amateur dog-fancier, purely by chance, achieved the highly successful cross that resulted in this nimble, intelligent breed. . . .' "

"Laugh," Kay told us calmly. "You'll see."

Purely as a sideline to puppy-raising, Kay launched her promised campaign to remove us from the pariah class—or as she chose to call us, accepting my title, The Unchosen. When we went into a huddle now it wasn't to gripe about

Ann Allison and other too obvious date-baiters, but to figure out how to emulate them.

First, the list.

"Look around you," Kay ordered, "wherever you are, and get more names. We've got to have absolute *quantities* before we start, so you don't die of discouragement if you don't connect first time up at bat. . . . That's all right, don't try to figure it out," she told Debbie hastily. "Just take my word for it, it'll work."

Debbie complied with hopeful eagerness, I with the unquestioning acceptance of a work-horse trudging its appointed round. For me Kay's campaign was just another bit of busyness, a time-filler, a project, like reading a daily page in the dictionary or cataloguing my books and records or learning how to knit—something to keep my mind occupied so there'd be no room for a vagrant thought; a stray, sad, aching "Why?"

When the final day of Christmas vacation had come and gone without glimpse or word of Norris—when the Sunday night supper dishes were carefully washed, and the Sunday night television programs carefully viewed, and the Sunday good nights carefully said, and the door of my room most carefully closed—then I'd cried. Soundlessly, a pillow over my head, the record-player volume turned up strong.

Sure, I'd joked New Year's Eve about Norris' defection, tried to pass it off to Mother and Dad with a so-what shrug— but right up to Sunday bedtime, a last wisp of hope had insisted that he'd come, he'd phone, there'd be some perfectly reasonable explanation of what had happened. How we'd laugh then about my doubts and anxieties! What silly jokes I'd tell him about the girls' suspecting I'd made him up! So said the small brave hope in a deep-down corner of my heart—

Till Sunday night. Then the hope curled up and died, and with it died my lovely secret world of romance. A world as fragile as tissue paper and rose-scented air. A gossamer shell cupped to hold love like a captured moonbeam. Now, as swiftly and mysteriously as it had flowered, it folded its petals tightly and withered to nothing.

The routine of classes again laid its pattern on my days. I came and went . . . went and came . . . to all appearances the same normal, unaltered Ellen Frazer (plus a few pounds, perhaps, and some color in her cheeks) seen at Easton before the Christmas holidays. Only I knew that the exterior was a phony, a human-like glaze on a wound-up doll whose hollow insides tick-tick-ticked . . . and felt nothing.

Then in midweek I came home from school to find an envelope in my mail, addressed in the familiar, heart-stopping, slanted print. For a shattering moment I saw skyrockets and a whirling blur of walls, windows, cupboards, and strangely tilted linoleum.

I sagged against the table, thankful for its support, grateful for the emptiness of the house, till I could manage the stairs. Behind the barrier of my own door I opened the envelope and drew out the single folded sheet.

The words ran together as had the kitchen walls and furnishings. "Awfully sorry . . . just couldn't make it . . . sure you'll understand . . . hope I didn't upset your plans too much . . . maybe some other time." Uneasy phrases barely filling a page, dreadful in their triteness.

I felt the solid door behind my back, heard myself say aloud, "I'm glad it wasn't an accident, or something." But was I? Tragedy would have thrown at least a tatterdemalion shred of dignity over the corpse that had been my love. I laid this letter away with the others in the miniature cedar chest.

But I couldn't lock up my scurrying thoughts as easily. What was the real reason behind those limp, lame excuses? Possibilities unrolled in my mind with the glib facility of a comic strip. He'd come to town—but cautiously, not announcing himself till he'd reconnoitered. He'd taken a quick peek at me—maybe on that dreadful day when Debbie had to pilot me home from Pete's—and that was enough to send him hightailing it back to California.

Or he'd happened on a student at his college who hailed from here. Perfectly natural that he'd be scouting around for passengers to share expenses of the trip. *Going to visit the Frazers in your town,* he'd have explained; *struck up quite a correspondence this past year with their daughter.*

In ruthless grisly detail my mind supplied the dialogue.
You don't mean Ellen?
Yes, do you know her?
Only by sight. You mean you've never met her? You're going up there on a sort of two-week blind date?
Well, yes, as a matter of fact. She certainly writes an entertaining letter. . . .
Writes—yes, quite an English hawk, as I remember. Sort of quiet—doesn't step out much—but probably a jewel of a girl. Not her fault that—
That what?
Now don't get me wrong—I'm just tipping you off that she is a bit on the dumpy side. The hausfrau type, you know. But what the heck—looks aren't everything—could be a heart of gold under those pounds of wienerschnitzel and apfelkuchen. . . .

Or he'd met a girl. A real live embodiment (not just a figment of words) of his imaginative soul-searching. I'd been only the dry run, the practice alert. Now he'd found her. Someone who, like me, shared his quirks of thought, his spirited fancies, his odd bits of philosophy—but who in addition had the advantage of proximity. A pretty girl—he was too romantic to be swept overboard by any other; dark, vivid, laughing, complex, a bewitching enigma, a heart-filling love. Yes, that was it. He'd met a girl.

No wonder I plunged with such desperate haste into any project that offered itself. So Kay wanted names, more and more names; doggedly, I added to my list:

Adam Jenkins (S; SB?).

Billy McNamara (PP; S).

Chuck Benson (P).

The names were meaningless, the entire campaign a child's soap bubble. So what? It was something to do while one day passed, two days, three . . .

Something to do till I no longer had to invent something to do.

Eighteen

Surround and infiltrate.

"Oh, thank you—" Debbie fluttered as Max Wilson lunged forward to pick up the book she had dropped. With an effort even I could detect, she added, "—Max."

He came up red-faced with the exertion required to fold himself into the narrow space between bus seats. Max was somewhat on the ponderous side. "'S'all right," he muttered, and riveted his gaze on the passing scenery.

Debbie rolled her eyes toward me in desperate appeal. I shook my head. Kay had forbidden us to sit together on the bus. We no longer met at my corner but got on separately, under orders *not* to dive for an empty seat but to sit with some other student.

"One of the boys on our list, if you can," Kay directed, "but otherwise *anybody*. Even a girl."

I felt strange and lost the first few days, standing alone at the bus stop. The three of us had been meeting on that corner for so long that we could time each other's arrival almost to the second. To walk down the road now by myself, to wait alone—conspicuously, awfully alone—for the bus to come was a new and disagreeable experience.

The first morning I stood solid as a watchtower on the Rhine, my eyes (like hooded lookout slits) fixed on a low-hanging branch across the road from which moisture dripped in cold, drizzling tears. My arms were cramped with the un-shifted weight of my books; my knees were locked so long in the same position that, when the bus finally arrived, they refused momentarily to flex, and I had to hobble aboard like someone on stilts.

The second morning I looked cautiously around and saw others also standing alone. My muscles imperceptibly relaxed; I began to feel less like a watchtower and more like a tree in a farmer's windbreak . . . not buddy-buddy with the next in line, you understand, but at least not a lonesome pine on the wide prair-ee.

On the third morning Ann Allison joined me.

"Hi, Ellen," she said with easy cordiality. "Where's Kay? And Debbie? Seems funny to see one of you without the others. Something happen? Big fight, maybe?"

"No, of course not." I flailed my mind for words. "Guess they got sick of sloshing over here when they can catch the bus right at home, practically."

"Hasn't the weather been *horrible?*" she agreed. "Sometimes makes me wish I were back East, bucking snowdrifts."

In surprise I asked, "Did you come from the East?" I'd thought of the Allisons as being here forever, like the three-hundred-year-old oak in front of the courthouse.

"Well, not *really* East—only you know how Oregonians call everything 'back East' from Colorado on! It was Minnesota actually. We moved out when I was in seventh grade. Dad absolutely couldn't take another blizzard; he had a sort of heart attack after shoveling out of the last one. . . ."

All I could say to that was "Oh." My mind had quit taking in facts after she said "seventh grade." I was remembering that the first year I'd really noticed Ann Allison was eighth grade at Taft when she'd been Pep Club president and Print and Cord Week Queen. ("Never fails—always the same kids," Kay and Debbie and I had pointed out cynically.) But at that time Ann had been almost a newcomer.

Shut off by my silence, Ann drifted over to join more congenial company. I got onto the bus, and still wordless, plopped down unseeingly by an equally silent seatholder. After a blank five minutes—reminded by Debbie's flutterings of Kay's directive—I took a quick sidewise glance and recognized my seatmate as Adam Jenkins.

So where did that leave me? He was in several of my classes, but we hadn't exchanged two words in our entire school life. With that as a background I could scarcely blurt out "Oh—you're Adam Jenkins, aren't you?" Nor could I drop a book, like Debbie; I just wasn't a book-dropper. I felt myself grow warm and red with my brain-beating efforts to think of something, anything, to say. Desperately I took another sidelong peek, hoping to find inspiration in his beaked profile—

And met his eyes as he peered warily at *me*.

127

In suffocating embarrassment I pivoted my full attention to the back of the driver's head and kept it there rigidly until our arrival at Easton released me.

In the hallway, bound for our lockers, I hissed at Kay, "I just can't *do* it! I *can't!*"

"Don't be silly. You're a writer, aren't you?"

"What's that got to do with it?"

"Write yourself some lines. Pretend the guy's a pen pal and you're dashing off a letter to him."

"I don't dash off letters," I admitted miserably. "I slave over them."

"Okay, *slave*, then! Just so you get something ready in advance." She stepped up her pace. "Go on—scram—you're cramping my style."

Forlornly I watched her stride down the hall ahead of me. Just short of her locker she caromed off a body taller and more ungainly than her own. "Oh, gosh, Loren—sorry!" she yelped in almost genuine dismay. The words were as graceless as her apologetic, stiff-armed wave that whammed a passing prof in the chest.

But at least she'd said them. She and Debbie were breaking the sound barrier. Why couldn't I? What was the *matter* with me?

In my room that night I brooded over the puzzle. For a year now *I'd* been the leading vote-getter for the title of Most Likely to Succeed in leaving the Unchosen. *I* was the one who had—well, practically—been going steady. Now it looked as though I'd be the one left home watching television while Kay and Debbie were off and running down the social track.

Why?

"It's because I don't really care," I defended myself. After all, my heart had just taken a tenth-round knockout. Under the same conditions Great-Great-Aunt Sophronia would have gone into a genteel decline, sitting home in a closely shuttered room, weeping gently into a lavender-scented hanky. While *I*—

While I was doing what? This hideaway of mine wasn't so very different from Aunt Sophronia's shadowed retreat, come to look at it. And though I could deny the lavender-scented hanky, I'd have to admit my stock of Kleenex was suspiciously low.

A decline. How *ridiculous!*

Furiously I pushed back from the desk and marched over to stare at myself in the mirror. Ordinarily I let my glance skim a mirrored surface like a skater avoiding thin ice, but not tonight. I stared belligerently at every detail.

My cheeks were again too pudgy (had I gained back *all* the weight I'd lost during those bleak steak-and-water days?); in profile I showed a dismaying double chin. Pale eyes. Mouth too full, its corners turned sulkily down under the weight of those apple-dumpling cheeks. Nose, insignificant. But—on the credit side—my skin was clear, and my hair (now that it had grown out a little on the sides) was more becoming than in its former bushwoman's mop.

I stood back from the mirror to assess further territory. Sloping, rounded shoulders. Too much stomach. Hips—oh, woe. I mounted a chair and continued the relentless survey. Heavy thighs. Bulging calves, only exaggerated by unexpectedly neat ankles.

Dejectedly I got off the chair, my spirits slumping lower than my shoulders. The total picture was pretty awful. . . .

But I'd looked at it. *Really* looked at it, seeing myself without illusion. What was it Kay said?—you can't solve a problem till you admit it exists?

All right, I was admitting it. My horrible pear-shape was

a problem. My round face was a problem. My strangling shyness was the worst problem of all. Never once in my life had I been interesting or clever or amusing, unless I was hiding behind a postage stamp.

There. I'd said it.

Now what could I do about it?

Nineteen

January was at midpoint when Kay decided the Unchosen were ready for step two. She called for a meeting after school in my room.

"I think—" she said, deliberately prolonging the moment to be sure she had our full attention, "now that we're on speaking terms with so many boys on our list, or at least a *couple* of us are"—her disparaging frown brushed me briefly —"it's time to give a party."

"Huh?"

"A *what?*"

"A party. Something casual like an open house or a cookout—if the rain ever stops—or a surprise party for one of our birthdays—"

"Nobody has a birthday in January!"

"How could it be a surprise if—"

"Well, we could pretend it was. The main point is to make it terribly informal, the come-as-you-are sort of thing, with everything provided by us so the boys won't be out a nickel. If we planned it for right after school, we could even offer 'em a ride."

"In what?"

"Oh, for pity's sake, in the family cars, that's what! Certainly our parents can do *that* much for us—after all, we're not asking for a debutantes' ball at the Ritz-Carlton!"

"You mean . . ." I said slowly, trying to believe what I'd heard, "that you're going to ask boys you've barely said hello to, to come to a *party?*"

Kay glowered at me. "And why not?"

"Why, because—because they won't come, that's all!"

"Some of them will. We don't expect a hundred percent return. As I've explained over and over again—"

"Don't do it again," Debbie begged hastily. "I get so confused. Do you honest and truly think it will work?"

"Of course it'll work. It's based on mathematics, isn't it? Then after they've come to *our* party, naturally they'll feel obligated to ask *us* to something. I figure that'll be the Valentine Mixer."

"Ohhhhh," Debbie's breath was expelled on a long, disbelieving sigh. "How do you know?"

"A simple matter of timing. If we give our party near the end of January, it'll be close enough to Valentine's Day so the boys'll just naturally think of the mixer as a good chance to pay us back."

"They will?"

"Really, Ellen," Kay's short span of patience had been stretched dangerously far, "if you know so much more about it, why don't *you* take over?"

"I don't want to take over. Maybe a party's a fine idea, only—"

"Only what?"

I took a deep, bracing breath. "Only I don't think we're ready for it yet."

"Maybe *you* aren't, but Debbie and I—"

"None of us. We've got lots of groundwork to do first. . . ."

"Like what?"

"Well, Debbie and I need to lose weight. . . ."

"Grief, Ellen, you've been all through that!" Kay cried crossly, while Debbie said, like a wounded deer, "You *know* I can't lose! I've tried and tried!"

"Not the right way. Not for long enough," I answered them both. "What we need is to find a *good* diet—something a doctor approves—and then *stay* on it."

"It won't make any difference," Debbie protested plaintively. "Not for me. Not with my glands. Why, my whole family—"

Like a bulldozer, I crunched remorselessly on my way. "Diet plus exercise. Next semester we ought to sign up for gym again . . ."

"*What?*"

". . . and send for one of those exercise programs to follow at home."

"Setting-up exercises." Debbie shuddered. "Oh, Ellen, there's nothing duller!"

"Not if we did them together. Kay, too. They'd build her

133

up while they're tearing us down. Probably improve her coordination."

"Now just a minute! There's nothing wrong with my—"

"Games, too." I stubbornly pursued the course I'd plotted during the long wakeful nights after my session with the mirror. "Sports are good exercise, and they might make us more graceful."

"If you mean me—" Kay sputtered.

"Then there's the sort of stuff you'd learn in a charm school," I drowned her out. "Like how to stand and walk. And sit down without falling apart."

"Ellen Frazer, I'm warning you—"

"Learning to make the best of your good points, and minimize the others. Finding out what clothes to wear, and how to do your hair. Watching your grooming, so you don't look sloppy. . . ."

"I don't have to sit here and be insulted—"

"Maybe we can't afford a charm school, but magazine articles give you a lot of the same tips. The thing is, if we work together we can criticize each other—"

"I've taken all the criticism I'm—"

"Because it's *awfully* hard to see yourself as you really are. We'd have to promise not to be tactful, but to say right out—"

Kay came to her feet with a crashing thump of chair legs that jolted my bulldozer to a startled halt. "You've said enough already," she told me coldly. "I'm doing just fine, thank you, without having to hear that I'm awkward and uncoordinated and sloppy and don't know what clothes to wear. And if you think you've helped Debbie's self-confidence any by telling her she's too fat—"

Debbie, unstrung by so bald an assertion, broke down and

wept. "I *kn-know* I am, but I didn't think my b-best friend would *say* so!"

"That's what best friends are for," I reminded her. "It was your other best friend who started this whole campaign."

"B-but that was different!" Debbie sobbed. "Kay never said I was—ohhhhh!" The three-letter word was too awful to repeat. She sobbed loudly.

"There, you see?" Kay said with satisfaction. "You've demoralized the poor girl. And just when our campaign was going so well! I half expected someone to ask her for a date *before* our party!"

Debbie looked up at her with streaming but hopeful eyes. "You did? Who?"

"Well, I don't like to say exactly *who,* but the way a couple of boys sit and moon at you in the bus"—Kay nodded with an oracle's mystic assurance—"I wouldn't be a bit surprised, that's all."

"Golly," murmured Debbie. The tears dried on her cheeks, leaving a faint salt trail. Her lips parted slightly. Her gaze, fixed on a fast-approaching future, was rapt. "You really think so?"

Studiedly they ignored me— Kay, because she didn't like interference; Debbie, because she didn't want to face disagreeable facts.

Well, I'd tried. Whether they went along with me or not, I was determined to launch my own step two. Maybe Kay was zooming down the homestretch; maybe her party would be the triumph she planned (knowing her, I didn't doubt it for a minute). But *I* wasn't ready yet for success—

Not till I had enough nerve to say hello to Adam Jenkins.

135

Twenty

I hadn't answered Norris' letter. What was there to say?

"I understand"—but I didn't.

"It's all right"—but it wasn't.

"Maybe some other time"—I couldn't make the hypocritical gesture.

But I tried. Evenings when I went to my room to study, I was drawn again and again to the desk with its open box of stationery, its waiting pen. Just a note—surely politeness demanded that much? Just a word to leave the door open— in case he wanted to write again, in case things changed. The wastebasket, filled with crumpled pale-gray balls, was emptied and filled again. When words and tone at last struck a delicate balance between common courtesy and hurt aloofness, pride made me crumple that effort, too. Anything I wrote would betray me; any arrangement of words would be a plea. No, I wouldn't write.

Only a year ago (my heart remembered) I'd been tiptoe with tingling excitement, dazzled, disbelieving, giddy with the prospect of each day's mail. Now the mail held nothing; I barely sifted through the thinning pile and seldom bothered to answer any of it.

Sometimes, in spite of my firmest resolutions, I spent a whole secret evening re-reading Norris' letters. They were so much more real and pulse-stirring, so much more intimately understanding than the labored conversations I managed occasionally now to launch into jerky motion.

"Hi—Adam."

"Oh . . . oh, hello."

"Kind of nice day, isn't it?—for a change."

"Yeh. For a change."

He was a *nothing*, I thought in despair; a thin, intense, gawky, wordless *nothing!* Why did I bother?

"Uh—I didn't get the science assignment—uh—Roger. I hate to bother you, but—"

"No bother. Here, it's all written down."

"Thanks—a lot. I'll just copy it—"

"Keep it. I've finished it already."

Indignantly I struck off the "S" before the "SB" in his code letters, thinking he needn't be so *obvious* about his superiority!

When the day's conversational efforts left me snarled in tight knots, it was pure relief to fling myself into the day's scheduled exercise. But other items in my new program were less pleasant.

The diet, for one. I'd approached Doctor Birkhart carefully, expecting prompt pooh-poohing of my request ("Stuff and nonsense! Where do all you young girls get the notion you're overweight?"). Instead he'd cooperated heartily. "Good idea! Ought to take off—mmm—twelve to fifteen pounds, I'd say. Make you feel much better. Brighter. Mentally alert."

Well! I left his office in a barely concealed huff. He could have protested a little bit—"You overweight? Oh, come now, Ellen!"

Mother more than made up for his lack of tact. "Not again!" she cried in alarm when I presented her with the diet list. "No, not when I just have you well and strong once more! David! David, you must stop her! Tell her this is foolishness—tell her how pretty she looks now, just as she is!"

"Mother, *Doctor Birkhart* says I should lose weight! He wrote out this diet himself."

"The man grows senile! His brains are addled! David, we must find a younger doctor while there is still time—"

"Now, Hilda, relax before you curdle," Dad soothed her. "This diet doesn't look too bad. Might do us all good to follow it awhile. . . ."

"Not you!" With passion Mother threw herself against this new threat. "How many years now have I tried to cover your poor bones! I can cook from dawn to dark and never put a pound on you!"

Dad winked at me gravely; I grinned my acknowledgment of the caloric red herring with which he'd drawn Mother off my trail.

Faithfully Mother prepared the foods on my list; in tight-lipped silence she served them (though her grimaces would have filled a thesaurus with uncomplimentary adjectives). And hungrily I ate them—right down to the last string bean and leaf of lettuce. For an age-long week I was *always* hungry; I woke at night from dreams of fluffy walnut cake with homemade ice cream, topping off a meal of barley-bean soup, veal chops, and sweet-potato *tzimmes*. One night I was so hungry I couldn't go back to sleep—I simply *had* to eat. My hand was on the doorknob when an idea stopped me.

I turned on the light, took my new red dress from the closet, and—for the first time since the dismal day I'd bought it—tried it on. The long zipper balked below my waistline. When I tried to pull the edges of material together, they didn't meet by a good two inches. I hung the dress from the arm of my floor lamp and went back to bed. There it still was—a mute reminder, when I weakened, of a goal to reach.

Eight endless days—and the worst was over. My stomach began to shrink (and my appetite with it); I was losing my craving for sweets. I could pull my belt a notch tighter. Even Debbie noticed.

"Gee," she said wistfully, "you're looking so *slim!* I wish I could lose."

"Go ahead, try," I urged her.

"It won't do any *good!*"

"Won't do any harm either."

She came home with me after school, and leafed through my exercise booklet. "These don't look so hard."

"They aren't a bit. And they only take twelve minutes a day."

She shook her head at my diet list. "Mom wouldn't make extra stuff just for me. She says it's enough trouble cooking one dinner."

"Why don't you try eating what the family has, only not so much? Little helpings, no dessert, nothing between meals?"

"Golly, it sounds—well, I could *try.*"

With more whole-souled interest she studied the impressive collection of clippings I was making from Mother's magazines (for once, I was thankful for Mother's magpie tendencies). She pored over hints on skin care, grooming, accessories. Soon after that, I noticed she'd given up spike heels with sportswear and exchanged her near-purple lipstick for a new pink-pearl. Her hair shone with brushing. Her hems and seams didn't so often show the silver glint of safety-pin repairs.

Kay, meanwhile, pursued her mathematically guaranteed objective. She announced one day that the party should be held the evening following our last final exam.

"For seniors it's the *final* final, see?" she pointed out. "Because we don't take exams our last semester. So there's our reason for throwing a party. A jubilee—hosanna—hail, hail, the gang's all here . . . that sort of thing. Only question now is where to have it. Not my house—you know how long anybody'd act free and easy *there,* with Mother swooping down on crumbs and wiping up tables."

"I suppose you could come to mine," Debbie began uncomfortably, "only—well—it isn't as though Tom and Polly'd *try* and crash it, but—"

The situation at the Fuller house was odd and more than a little sad. To all appearances Debbie was the perfect big sister, interested and amused and tender over Polly's premature blooming. But nobody could mistake the raw hurt envy underneath. All that kept Debbie's jealousy tamped down was her trust in Kay's campaign. Once she herself was dating, she could take Polly's conquests in stride. But in the meantime—

"Why don't you hold it at my house?" I suggested quickly. "I'll have to check with Mother, but you know how she is—

she'll probably bless you for giving her somebody to cook for."

"Swell. Don't let her think we'll dump it *all* on her though. Once we figure out our menu, we'll divide it three ways—"

"Oh, sure!" Debbie agreed, her enthusiasm underscored with relief. "Mom would be *tickled* to fix stuff for us—you just say what!"

So it was arranged. So, by our three diverse routes—Kay homing in on the clean, pure, undeviating highroad of mathematics; I struggling up the bur-studded, hilly path of self-improvement; Debbie wafting in on a rainbow of hope—we approached what was surely the strangest gathering ever to be given the name of jubilee.

Twenty-one

"Oh—hey, Chuck—you know what?" With grim stubbornness I had rehearsed the casual invitation. I'd written it out first; I'd memorized it; over and over and over, last night, I'd practiced the light, easy tone. Now here I was, fumbling my lines like a novice ingenue paralyzed by the footlights.

The big, raw-boned, stoop-shouldered boy had stopped at my call and was looking at me warily. I flung myself into the balance of my speech, punctuating it with awful cackles supposedly representing light laughter.

"A gang of us are getting together at my house tonight to celebrate, you know, no more finals for us seniors after today —we're done with all that! Want to come?"

I could almost see his mental gears shifting from low to second as he labored to put together a refusal. Any moment now he'd mutter something and escape. I hurried on.

"The more the merrier, you know! It's going to be lots of fun—loads to eat; Mother's already got the house smelling like a bakery—she'll be so disappointed if there's a scrap left over—"

This portion of the invitation was written in specially for Chuck, whose bony body gave the impression of never having surrounded a full meal. I saw him hesitate; shrilly I pursued my advantage.

"Don't bother to dress—everybody's coming in school clothes. Any time after seven—okay? See you then!"

I'd got through it! After that our escape was mutual. Chuck plunged into a between-classes surge of kids; I ducked for the girls' lounge to take half a dozen deep breaths. My heart was going full gallop, tantivy-tantivy. I *couldn't* do it again. I couldn't! The buzzer for next class went off like a rattlesnake above my head. I spurred through the door into the speeding pack and found myself racing alongside Roger Austen.

"Oh—hey, Roger—you know what?"

By midafternoon, I had stumbled through my script four times, received one scared "NO!" two "Well-uhs," and a doubtful acceptance, "If I can make it before too late. I've got a sort of meeting first."

Somewhat forlornly I submitted my results to Kay and Debbie and found theirs equally dubious.

"What do we do now? How many do we get ready for?" I added bleakly, "If any."

Debbie looked from one to another of us in scared appeal. "What do you mean, if any? Don't you think *anybody*—"

"Of course *somebody'll* come," Kay assured her heartily.

"Not everybody. That's why we had to ask so many. I'd figure on about—mmm—say, forty percent. That's five and a half . . ."

"Which one's the half?" I asked. "Stuart Schofield?"

She ignored my attempt at humor. "Let's say, five or six. A very reasonable return, with a good margin for error, since even three would be enough."

"Gee, six boys!" Debbie, inevitably, seized on the figure offering maximum hope.

"If that many come, though," Kay tapped her teeth with her pencil, new concern wrinkling her forehead, "we'll be awfully unbalanced. And it'd look kind of obvious, too. I mean, any boy there, even the *dumbest,* would see what we were up to. What we've got to do is invite some girls!"

"Oh, *no!*" wailed Debbie.

"Oh, *yes!* You two ask the first senior girls you run into this next period. Time's getting short—so *do* it!"

I agreed silently with Debbie; it was a stupid idea. If Kay's precious computer went haywire, we might end up with all the girls accepting and only a single boy! Good grief, wouldn't that be something? Half a dozen hens clucking over a lone rooster! The poor guy'd be scared out of his tail-feathers!

Glumly I chugged toward my last scheduled exam, English lit. Who was I supposed to invite, for Pete's sake? Kay should have thought of this earlier. We had no girls on our list of names. Anyway, nobody but oddballs and duds would come to a party we gave; the others would know it was social suicide.

"Don't *scowl* so, Ellen! If you're scared of English lit, I'm panicked!"

It was Ann Allison laughing back at me as she passed on

her way to the exam. My response was purely mechanical. After all, I'd said the words so often, aloud and to myself, in the last twenty-four hours that they practically constituted my day's vocabulary. Ann's greeting merely tripped the record.

"Oh—hey, Ann—you know what?"

After school, Kay and Debbie pinned my ears back. "You *idiot!* Why *her?*"

"You said to ask the first senior girl we ran into. . . ."

"But not *her!* What do we want with a big wheel like that?"

"Shucks, she won't come," I defended myself. "She was just being polite. Bet she's on the phone, soon as she gets home, to say something came up and she's awfully sorry and all that." It had jolted my mental needle clear out of its groove when Ann Allison had replied, "What fun! I'd love to come!" After a shock like that it's a wonder I'd even *passed* the exam, let alone get my expected *A!*

"She'd better not come," Kay glowered. "Honestly, if I'd known you'd be such a *stupe—*"

"Nobody will look at us," Debbie mourned, "if *she* shows up."

"Well, she won't, so forget it. . . . Who'd *you* ask?"

"Mary Ralston," Debbie announced with pride, "because she's going steady, so I knew—anyway, she asked if she could bring Jim, so we're sure of *one* boy, even if he is taken."

"Very smart. Really using your head," Kay approved. "I asked Pam Scott and Margie Eckleberg. They said they'd come."

I'll bet, I thought. *Probably gobbled the invitation like seal swallowing fish.* If anybody was more on the outer fringe than us, it was Pamela and Margie.

145

"Well, let's get on with it." Kay was again in command, issuing crisp directives. "Lots to do before seven o'clock!"

At home I found Mother anxiously surveying the living room. "Is it all right, Ellen?" she asked. The house smelled like heaven. My diet-shrunken stomach reeled back on the ropes, crying for mercy. By some legerdemain Mother had created a look of space in our over-crowded living room. Furniture had been pushed back or was missing entirely.

"It looks marvelous," I praised her. "If anybody comes, they'll love it."

"If any—"

"Just a manner of speaking. . . . Golly, with all this room we can have a buffet!"

"A—yes?"

"Across the end here." I got our two card tables from the hall closet and set them up side by side. "Sure! It'll look great." And allow us to exhibit the food early and often, I added to myself, since it was our main item of entertainment.

"But not the old table, Ellen!" Mother's face puckered with anxiety. "So bad it looks—let me run next door and borrow Mrs. Markey's!"

"Who's going to see it? With a cloth over it, it looks as good as the new one." I went out to check the kitchen; it was almost too much to bear—those gorgeous cakes— "Mother, you shouldn't have baked *two!*"

"It was no trouble. And boys—ach, they have no bottom!"

I peeked into refrigerator and bread box. "Gosh, with all Kay and Debbie are bringing, we could feed an army. Poor Dad will have to eat turkey sandwiches and honey cookies for *weeks!*"

"Ah, no, you'll see! Boys"—Mother spread her hands in an all-encompassing gesture—"a mountain they could eat their way through, and come out hungry! I *know!*"

I retreated to the bathtub, unable to dampen her enthusiasm with further warning of the total who might actually show up to devour her goodies. There was always Mary Ralston's Jim, I remembered hopefully.

Kay and Debbie arrived soon after six-thirty. They added their loaded baskets of provender to the buffet (now splendidly covered with a big bright dinner cloth that touched the floor on both sides); the resulting picture was magnificent and awesome, something like the original Thanksgiving, or the horn of plenty at harvest festivals. Even Mother was satisfied with its look of abundance.

Once the buffet was arranged, we had nothing to do but wait. Nervously. Tensely. The tall old grandfather's clock announced the hour sonorously. Dad picked up his newspaper and said genially, "Well, better get out of here." Mother followed him into the study. The three of us remaining exchanged uneasy glances.

And waited.

One minute, two, three—how loudly the clock ticked! Four, five. At ten minutes past the hour, I went over and stopped the noisy pendulum. I didn't dare look at the buffet. All that food—how could I live with Mother's and Dad's tactful disposal of it? With their *pity?* Twelve minutes, thirteen . . .

The doorbell rang. All three of us sprang to our feet. Then Debbie and Kay sat down hastily in deference to my prior rights as hostess. I stumbled across the expanse of floor, silently rehearsing my newest script—"Oh, he*llo!* So nice you could come!—"

The doorknob slipped under my damp grasp. I wiped my hand on my skirt and tried again. My smile was permanently frozen in place. My record was already playing, "Oh, he*llo*—" as I swung open the door.

Twenty-two

Margie Eckleberg and Pamela Scott stood on the porch. Like puppets jerked into simultaneous motion by the door's opening, each girl promptly extended a covered plate.

"Cookies," they spoke together, and then, peering past me into the quiet house, "are we too early?"

Their coldly indignant glances crossed. *I told you it was too soon,* each accused the other. *I told you we'd be the first.*

"No, no, you're not a *bit* early," I assured them with loud insincerity. "Come in, come in!" I accepted the plates, wondering what on earth to do with them. "Cookies! How lovely!"

"Raisin and chocolate chip," explained Pamela.

"We just thought they might come in handy," Margie amplified.

"In case more kids came than you expected," Pamela finished the little speech. It was reassuring to know that others also prepared scripts in advance.

I gestured the girls in with a welcoming elbow, then leaped ahead to the living-room door, squawking in loud warning to Kay and Debbie, "Look what Margie and Pam brought! Cookies! Isn't that *nice?*"

My entrance was too precipitate. I tripped on the rug. Two cookies shot out from beneath their wax-paper shield and hit the floor; before I could stop myself, I'd tramped one into crumbs.

"Good grief—how clumsy can I get! I'm so *sorry!*"

"The rug—oh, dear—" Kay rushed for broom and dustpan.

"Hey, look out! There goes another!" Debbie snatched the tilting plates from my hands.

Margie said wretchedly, "The plates were too full."

Again the exchange of accusing glances: *I told you they were too full. It was your idea to pile them up like that.*

"Oh, that isn't so—not at all—it's just awkward old me!" I swooped for the unbroken cookie as Kay began whisking up crumbs around my feet. "Anyway, we only lost one. Look, this is good as new!"

"It's been on the floor—"

"Who cares? I'll eat it myself!"

"You don't have to do that—just throw it away."

"Wouldn't dream of it!" I protested in awful jollity, chewing vigorously. "Mmmm, *good!*"

Debbie, standing at the buffet with a plate in each hand,

149

said helplessly, "Will somebody come move something? There's no room."

Pamela and Margie looked at the groaning (or anyway, creaking) board, and then at each other. *I told you it was a stupid idea to bring cookies. I told you they wouldn't want them.*

I choked in my haste to interrupt the silent, malevolent dialogue. "Why, there's lots of room. We sort of spread things out so it'd look like more!" Heedless of the pretty arrangement Debbie had worked out, I shoved dishes together. My foot struck a leg of the older card table; the loaded surface slanted delicately toward one corner. "Oops! There I go again!" I laughed heartily as I kicked the leg back into place. "Pretty soon we'll *all* be eating off the floor!"

What time was it? For how many hours had I been making these ghastly gay noises? Why didn't Kay or Debbie *say* something?

The doorbell rang.

Automatically I readied my frozen smile, my prepared script, as I lunged across the intervening space to fling open the door. "Oh, hel*lo!* So nice you could come!"

It was Mary Ralston and her Jim. Mary held out a plate. "I brought a few cookies, just in case."

"Cookies!" I screamed. "How *wonderful!* Come *in!* Look, Debbie, Kay—more cookies! Isn't that marvelous?"

A car turned noisily into the driveway. Boys' voices shouted above the slam of doors. Suddenly I came utterly unstrung. I looked to Kay for help; she was already at the buffet, scowling in her effort to create room for Mary's offering. Debbie?—but Debbie sat paralyzed, her eyes bigger than Mother's blueberry pies. The doorbell rang.

I thrust the cookies back into Mary's hands. "Well! Who's

here *now?*" I shouted, struggling to regain my cheery tone and only just stopping short of a strangled "Ho, ho, ho!" like a department-store Santa on the verge of Christmas-Eve laryngitis.

I made it to the door on feet more frozen than my smile. "Oh, hel*lo!* So—"

The porch fairly teemed with boys! Boys shoving, pushing, haw-hawing. Boys obviously banded together more for mutual support than the need of transportation.

"—nice you could come," I finished weakly, my shout reduced to a wisp of breath. How many were there? Four—five—they were milling around too much; I couldn't count.

The focus of confusion was revealed when a stubby figure erupted from the melee, pushed by many hands. Max Wilson. With bulldog pertinacity he gripped a slightly smashed paper plate. "Cut it out now! Lea' me alone! Quit shovin'!"

"G'wan! Give it to her!"

"His maw made 'im bring cookies—"

"We had a heck of a time keepin' him from eatin' 'em all."

"Waddya mean, *me?* It was you guys alla time grabbin' for 'em!" Max shoved the plate at me. "Some of 'em need brushin' off."

"Oh, *thank* you!" I managed, and stepped back to avoid the surge of bodies. Not really so many—it was just the combined poundage that overwhelmed me. Plus petrifying surprise. Till that moment I hadn't really expected one boy to show. Billy McNamara, Max, Bill Whitaker (I tallied them with disbelief as they surged toward the living room), Stuart Schofield, Chuck Benson, two boys I didn't know . . .

Another car stopped. I waited to greet Loren Marsh with a shaky "Hel*lo!* So nice—" before following them all to the living room.

151

Debbie's face was absolutely luminous. Pamela and Margie —their silent dialogue stilled—sat in stiff anguished shyness, hands folded tightly in their laps. Kay, even as she muttered hello, was frowning at the fresh problem presented by Max's cookies. We both went over to the buffet to move dishes. The boys trooped after us.

"Hey, looky that *food!*"

Kay blocked them off with scoutmaster efficiency. "Not yet —hold on! Have to wait'll everybody comes."

Who else could she possibly expect? Her computer had already blown its neat mathematical top, and was spouting astronomical figures. What were we supposed to do with them all? My wildest pre-party hopes had exploded no further than the possibility of each girl entertaining a single boy.

The boys, driven from the buffet, retreated to the record player. Frowning, they sifted through our collection of long-plays.

"This all ya got, hey?" Bill complained.

Loren shushed him. "What d'ya expect? Rock 'n' roll? This stuff's *good.*" He put on an old Lehmann recording of German *lieder,* a favorite of Mother's. Looking at the other boys' faces, I thought I'd just simply die.

The doorbell rang. *I won't answer it,* I thought. *This is turning out awful. It'll never end. I don't want anybody else to come.* I covered the distance to the door, preparing my horrible smile, my Bluebeard's greeting, "Oh, he*llo!* . . ."

Then my mind reeled like an off-course gyroscope. Norris stood outside the door. . . .

No, not Norris. A trick of the dim porch light. The almost-same profile. "So nice you could come!" I ushered Adam Jenkins into the living room, and for a necessary minute leaned dizzily against the wall.

152

"Psst!" Kay hissed at me. "What time is it?"

"How do I know?" I wasn't wearing my watch. The clock showed a perpetual 7:10.

"Can't be anybody else coming!" It should have been gratifying to see The Brain looking so harassed over her misbehaving statistics, but I was too upset myself. "Lots more here already than ever should have come! Maybe we'd better let them eat."

"Oh, gosh, Kay, *then* what?" A whole evening on our hands—nothing to do. "Better hold 'em off a *little* longer!"

"Look at 'em . . . we've got to do *something!*"

With the boys' arrival the party had split down the middle. Even Mary's Jim had deserted her to join the male huddle at the far end of the room. Mary had moved over to sit on the couch with Debbie and Pam and Margie, her rigid smile indicating this wasn't at all to her liking. Kay and I stood guard over the buffet. Loren alone remained at the record player, listening to the rich, dark, intensely poignant tones, punctuated with growing frequency by the boys' guffaws. Suddenly Billy (where had we ever got the idea he was shy?) launched out in competition with Lehmann. *"Ach, du lieber Augustine . . ."*

He was an instant hit. The boys roared. The girls smiled in pained acquiescence to masculine humor.

"Shut up!" ordered Loren.

"Oh, yeh?" Backed by unaccustomed support and cocky with success, Billy had become a swaggerer. "Who's gonna make me?"

Loren advanced on him. Billy pressed backward into the huddle which promptly rebounded him to meet his towering adversary. The girls on the couch squealed. The record reached the spot where the needle invariably stuck. *"Mein liebes Kind,"* the stirring voice repeated urgently, *"mein liebes Kind, mein liebes Kind, mein—"*

"*Ach, du lieber Augustine!*" shrilled Billy in defiant answer.

Loren swung—and missed. Debbie screamed. I took an instinctive backward step and kicked the card-table leg again. Kay, behind the table, yelped a warning. Like an imponderable glacier advancing over a helpless land, the heaping plates of food began a slow slithering descent toward the weakened corner. Kay and I grabbed the table to hold it level; my foot searched beneath the tented cloth for the bent leg.

"Where is it? What happened to the fool thing?"

Kay lifted the cloth to peer underneath the table.

The doorbell rang.

Twenty-three

Like a mouse in a maze, reacting automatically to the bell's summons, I turned from table to door. Kay made a gargling sound; I didn't stop to interpret it. Loren and Billy, fists cocked, were engaged in a cautious circling maneuver.

"Go get 'im!" yelled Chuck. "Don't let 'im scare ya, just 'cause he's twice as big!"

The others shouted at his witticism.

"Jim, stop them!" squealed Mary.

"Mein liebes Kind, mein liebes Kind, mein liebes—" pleaded the magnificent voice on the record.

"Help!" called Kay, her voice curiously muffled. "Somebody *help!*"

The uproar was ghastly. So was my smile as I opened the door. "He*llo!* So nice—" I couldn't finish.

Ann Allison and Roger Austen stood there smiling at me. "Are we awfully late?" asked Ann. "I forgot about the meeting, but Roger said *he'd* told you, so I didn't call." She held out a covered plate; I stared at it dumbly. "Just a few cookies. I know how these open-house things can get away from you—somebody brings somebody else, and suddenly—"

I stepped back, not offering to take the plate. Roger followed Ann to the living room. I dragged along in the rear, a reluctant participant in a gruesome nightmare. The din was awful. Why didn't Dad or Mother come out and stop it? Why didn't the floor give way and drop the whole abominable, shouting, shoving crew into the basement? I never wanted to lay eyes on any of them again—not even Kay and Debbie. With Ann Allison's appearance as witness to the debacle, my humiliation was complete.

Or so I thought. There was more to come.

"Ellen—Debbie—somebody for gosh sakes, *help!*"

The voice came from beneath the buffet. I took a second, disbelieving look and saw Kay's orange head draped in a babushka of tablecloth. That was all we needed—the final comic touch.

Furiously, unreasoningly angry, I demanded, "Good grief, what are you doing under there?"

"What d'you *think* I'm doing? Holding up the blasted table! You *dropped* it on me!"

Unexpectedly Ann's laughter rang out like a carillon of bells on Sunday morning . . . so natural, so spontaneous, so engaging that it first startled the room into silence, then produced sputtering echoes as others saw the reason for it.

Debbie, Mary, Chuck, and Jim ran to support the loaded

table. Loren turned from battle to lift the needle from the record and give Lehmann blessed release. Billy, grinning sheepishly, stuffed his fists in his pockets. Kay crawled out from beneath the table, grumbling, "Of all the fool things to do! Run off and leave me holding up a ton of food! I was scared to budge for fear the whole darn thing'd collapse."

Ann cried, "It *is* a ton of food—at *least* a ton! Oh, isn't it magnificent? And here I brought *more!*" This time the chiming melody was directed against herself. Others joined in. And still others. The room rocked under waves of sound, more deafening than before.

Only now, somehow, it wasn't appalling. The roars of laughter unlocked tension, embarrassment, self-consciousness. Suddenly everybody began to talk at once. Even Pamela and Margie burst into loud animated chatter. I listened incredulously. In twinkling seconds the near-fight was becoming a Paul Bunyan legend; the near-disaster to our feast, a subject for a Pulitzer prize cartoon. I heard myself joining in, embroidering the awful incidents with new absurdities . . . and I heard the note of hysteria in my laughter.

From time to time I stole cautious glances at Adam Jenkins, trying to catch the same semi-profile view that had so unnerved me at the door. I couldn't recapture it. Adam didn't look a bit like Norris. I must be losing my mind.

Beneath my shrill laughter, my shouted invitation—"Better come eat, everybody! Table's sinking, and Kay won't get under it again!"—I felt hollow and aching. Must I always look for Norris? Could I never lay his ghost?

Roger said, "Hey, I've got some records in the car—anybody heard that crazy sound track where they left in all the goofs?"

A dozen voices urged him to bring it in. To the clink of

china and silver, and the laughter and chatter, was added a singing voice that quite often broke off to scream in outrage at the quality of its performance.

The singer was followed by a howling parody on famous holiday songs. Then a rattling, rousing dance band. A couple of the bolder boys seized partners and whirled them out to the kitchen's waxed linoleum. Roger asked, "Hey, how about it?" And before I could protest that I didn't dance, I was convoluting as madly as the rest—with no clear idea of *what* I was doing, but in that cheerful chaos, what difference did it make?

Kay remained at the buffet to serve and to replenish supplies from the store in the kitchen as, unbelievably, they ran low. Her freckled angular face was pale with excitement and concentration; her voice, like mine, was pitched several notes above normal. I looked around for Debbie and didn't see her. Later, dancing—or hopping—with Max Wilson, I was steered out of the crowded kitchen down the uncarpeted length of shadowy back hall—

And into a very quiet couple who broke apart with a startled leap.

Debbie said, "Oh!" Her cheeks were very pink; her eyes, very round and bright. Billy McNamara said nothing.

"Well, well, *well!*" Max commented, and tactfully hopped me out of their vicinity.

The party broke up around midnight when—to my utter surprise—we actually ran out of food. Incredible that that bountiful heap—plus all Mother's extras—was someplace inside the still-noisy crowd that yelled good-byes, honked and roared motors, and—at last—left us to the job of cleaning up. Mother and Dad had long ago slipped out of the study and up to bed. The strident record player was silent.

We three looked at the litter of dirty dishes, crumpled paper napkins, oddments of potato chips, pickle stems, olive pits, sandwich crusts, and then—warily—at each other. At the same moment we all hurried into shrill comment.

"What a smash!"

"Wasn't it *marvelous?*"

"Absolutely utter!"

"Look at Debbie—she's still in orbit!"

"You mean still out in the hall with Billy McNamara!"

"Stop it, you two!"

"How many *came?* Seemed like hundreds!"

"I'd never have believed it—aren't mathematics *wonderful?*"

"That's what I've been telling you all along—just a matter of pure calculation—"

Nobody spoke of the party's dreadful beginning. Nobody hinted that it was a dismal, foundering failure—till the last guests arrived.

Nobody mentioned Ann Allison at all.

Twenty-four

The party was a success, we agreed. A triumph for mathematics and holding the good thought.

Only—its results were as bouncy as a deflated beachball. Our phones and doorbells continued silent. Nobody called, nobody dropped in to suggest a ride or a show or a soda at Pete's, let alone sign us up for the Valentine Mixer. The few days of midterm vacation passed; we went back to Easton, no better off than before.

Except that now, when we crossed paths with our one-time guests, we didn't have to invent conversation. They spoke first.

"Hey, sure hadda swell time 'tyour house." (Max)

"Real fun, that night. Real food, too—wow!" (Chuck)

"Certainly enjoyed the get-together." (Loren) "Meant to call and say thanks, but—"

"Uh—some fun, huh?" (Adam, wordless as ever. But how did I know he wasn't thinking deep thoughts, phrasing inner imaginings that shyness held captive?)

"Adam—do you—did you ever have a pen pal?"

"Huh?"

"You know . . . somebody you wrote letters to? A friend who moved away, or—or—"

"Gosh, *letters?* Bad enough all the school stuff we gotta write!"

(Scratch Adam. Quit trying to force him into Norris' mold, just because for one moment he stood where Norris might have stood and looked as Norris might have looked.)

"Oh, say, wasn't it fun?" (Ann) "Such a *good* idea—let's do it again soon!"

"Yes." *Over my dead body,* I added silently. I hated Ann for saving the party from grisly failure. I hated her particularly because I didn't know how she'd done it.

"Ellen—" Ann had fallen into step with me; I walked faster but couldn't shake her. "I've been wanting to ask you—Kay and Debbie, too—" (*Now what office was she running for?* I armored myself against the upcoming request.) "Are any of you interested in Junior Achievement?"

Junior Achievement was just a name to me, one of the thirty-nine activities open to John Eastoners. I knew it vaguely as a learn-by-doing sort of thing: Kids organized actual business firms that produced and sold goods or services. "Well, no . . . that is, I don't think—"

"I've got to drop out this semester; Thespians meets the

same night. Isn't it awful—all the conflicts? Pretty soon we'll be double-shifting the extra-curries! Anyway, I promised Roger I'd try to get someone in my place—we've got a real good company going; it's tops in sales. Of course, maybe you're booked up Tuesday nights, too?"

I wasn't booked for any night, and she knew it. "Sorry."

"Maybe Kay—"

I veered off rudely, leaving her question in midair.

By the middle of the week Debbie's anxiety spilled over into words. "What went wrong?" she demanded of Kay. "What do we do *now?*"

"Nothing went wrong," Kay assured her. "We made a fine start. Of course, it *is* just a smidgen late to be starting. If we'd done this our sophomore year—"

"But we *didn't!* You mean now it's too late?"

"Of course not. Don't panic—I'll think of something. Just keep looking around for more names to add to the list; we're bound to turn up somebody sometime. It's a mathematical certainty."

Debbie's gaze was despairing. Mathematics had so far proved no cure-all, nor had simple hope; her rainbow had touched ground in a briar patch.

I tried to interest her again in my own program. "Look how well you're doing! You lost two pounds last week."

"So what's two pounds?"

"Well, it proves you *can* lose weight! If you'd come do exercises with me—"

"Ugh."

I often felt the same way about them. About the whole program, for that matter. Ugh. Up, down, over, around—brush, brush, till my arms ached (hair, clothes, shoes)—shower, shampoo, launder (I was so clean, I squeaked)—set pin curls, manicure nails, rub in lotions, sew on buttons, press blouses—and what did it get me? Praise from Dad— "Well, what a bonny lass we have this morning!" Grudging approval from Mother—"The diet is perhaps not *too* bad." Slow, slow changes in my list of secret statistics—"Weight, –7. Waist, –2. Stomach, –3¼. Hips, –2½."

Grimly I held to my appointed course through January's soggy days. Whatever its other results, the program was a time filler. An evening filler. Its multitude of requirements prevented my dipping into the little cedar chest (too often), or brooding over my box of pictures (I always ended in tears). Most important, it gave me no time to write a letter that pride would no longer have kept me from mailing.

Where Norris was concerned, I was fresh out of pride. What difference if he'd let me down, embarrassed me horribly before family and friends?—I didn't *care*. Just so he'd write again. Just so my day could again build up to the moment when I snatched up the mail and hurried to my hideaway . . . to lose myself in his letter . . . to know my dreams were mirrored, my inner poetry echoed, in another heart . . . to spend long hours composing an answer in words as deeply meaningful, as expressively beautiful, as his. Compared to all I'd lost, pride was a poor thing.

But somehow I hung onto its shredding hem—with the help of those many, many little squares to be filled with an "X" before I could call a day complete (up, down, brush, shower, mend, press). It was a disappointment, though, that the party hadn't produced something more entertaining in the way of distractions.

Second semester I signed up for gym. Kay and Debbie thought I'd gone out of my mind and said so. "You'd better watch it—you'll turn into one of those repulsive outdoor types, all muscle and good cheer, dogtrotting down the highway—"

"You're the one doing the dogtrotting. . . . How are the Tergles?"

"Oh, swell, you've got to come see them! They can all eat from a dish now—and the way they tuck into that pablum! Slurp, slurp, the floor's practically spatter-painted in oatmeal-gray before they're through!"

"What floor?"

"Why, the back entry! Good grief, you didn't think we'd leave new pups outdoors in weather like this—they'd drown! Besides, now they're being weaned, it's more convenient; who wants to stand out in the rain four times a day to feed them?"

"*Four* times—I haven't seen you zipping home at noon—"

"Well, I did. Anyway, once. Mother said it was silly, and besides, then *I* didn't get any lunch. So she feeds them."

I repeated incredulously, "Your—mother—feeds—the—puppies?"

"Sure. What's so hard about that? I measure out their formula before I leave. All she's got to do is mix it together—"

My imagination boggled. I simply could not picture the immaculate Mrs. Nicholson in her immaculate back entry . . . well, her *once* immaculate back entry—

And here was Kay, reacting as calmly as though it were another of her mathematical certainties!

Maybe it was. Maybe it could even be reduced to a formula. "Expose one thwarted mother—" (wouldn't any mother of a thorny touch-me-not like Kay feel thwarted?) "—to four velvet-eared puff-balls, requiring large daily quantities of pablum laced with the milk of human kindness and interspersed with frequent cuddling—"

164

Kay was right. Mathematics *could* be fascinating.

My insistence on taking gym threw our schedules out of kilter. Running through my first week's classes, I was a little dismayed to see how few I shared now with Kay and Debbie. Well, all the more chance to get new names for the list—including girls. No telling when Kay would have another brainstorm; I wasn't going to be caught short again with only Ann Allison to ask—never!

"Uh—hello . . . Julie."

"Oh, hi." (I pretended not to see her swift glance at my notebook cover.) "Ellen. What d'ya think of old Stanton? He sounds pretty rugged."

"He isn't, though—really. I had him last year. He just starts out that way."

"Hey, good to know! I'm breathing easy."

I wasn't. Why was it always so suffocatingly hard to speak to people? Why must I always stammer and blush and choke with embarrassment? Maybe I just wasn't the type to make friends—except in letters. Maybe I ought to give up—send for a new list of pen pals . . .

"Uh, hi—Pat. Looks like we drew Miss Heller again."

"Isn't it awful? Guess we don't live right." (Again the quick glance at the name on my notebook.) "Ellen. Good people go to heaven, but sinners go to Heller." The big girl laughed in hearty approval of her joke. "And here I thought I was earning brownie points like mad—"

"What are brownie points?"

"You mean you weren't ever a brownie scout? Good deeds, that's what! And have I been piling 'em up! Sunday school, Epworth League, Peppermint-Sticking. . . ."

"Peppermint—what?"

"Oh, that's working at the hospital. We wear red-and-white striped seersucker; the kids call us Peppermint Sticks."

"You mean you're a—a nurse's aide?" Awe made me gargle the question.

"Gosh, no! The mortality rate up there'd be awful! We just do odd jobs . . . serve dinner trays, push around the book cart. Girls in League chose it for our civic service this year. Last year we visited shut-ins—arrgh!—I had to read to a deaf old guy who wouldn't have anything but Shakespeare. Can you imagine shouting 'O Romeo, Romeo' into an *ear trumpet?* Oops, here's Heller."

Just listening to Pat left me slightly winded. How did some people *do* it? Their words rippled along like a creek dancing over stones, while mine were snaggled tighter than sticks in a beaver dam.

"Hullo—uh—Joan."

"Oh—hi." (No sidelong glance at my notebook.)

"Kind of a small class—for a change. Can't be more than fifty!" A feeble joke—but for me pretty sensational.

"Yes."

Utterly squelched, crimson-eared, I retreated into concentrated note-taking. Couldn't win all the time (I tried to lift my flattened morale); bound to be a few snobs who felt no compulsion to be polite to the class zero. Scratch Joan. Forget about her. Go on to the next one.

I couldn't. It was too hard at best. I finished the day with gruff monosyllables.

Only Kay was waiting at the bus-loading exit.

"Where's Debbie?"

Kay's expression became slightly complacent. "Debbie? Oh, Debbie got a ride home. With Billy McNamara."

"She *didn't!* You're kidding!"

"Don't know why you're so surprised. That was the whole purpose of the party, wasn't it?"

166

"Oh, come off it— What happened?"

Kay confessed, "I don't really know. I was down at my locker when she came tearing past, looking like a kid seeing his first elephant, and said, 'Don't wait for me—Billy's giving me a ride home.' "

"You must have seen them together—"

"N-no. Not *really*."

"But you've noticed *something*—"

"Well, only that Debbie sort of hangs around his locker —I mean, I *guess* it's his locker, because it certainly isn't hers. . . ."

"Well, I'll be swizzled!" Mathematics and hope. Look what they could do for you.

Silently we boarded the bus. Silently—each thinking her own thoughts—we rode the long way home.

Twenty-five

Eager for an explanation I phoned Debbie's house as soon as I got home.

"She's not here yet, Ellen," Mrs. Fuller reported. "I was just going to call *you* to say if she's over there, send her right home. I simply *have* to have an extra pair of hands if I'm to get these dishes back on the shelves before time to start supper. My, the way housework gets away from me is dreadful! It's my glands, you know; I just don't have the energy I should. Now today I bit off more than I can chew—set out to put fresh paper on all the kitchen shelves. So here I am with the job half done, and dishes all over the counter and stove and table, and nobody to help me in my weakened condition—DEBBIE! IS THAT YOU?— No, it's just Tom. Now where was I?"

"Putting the dishes away," I said hurriedly. "Sorry to have bothered you. G'bye."

Whether Mrs. Fuller didn't mention that I'd phoned, or Debbie chose not to call me back, I didn't know. The evening passed, leaving my curiosity unappeased.

Nor did I learn much the following day. Debbie wasn't exactly evasive, but she was harder to pin down than a cricket. I understood what Kay meant about her looking like a kid seeing his first elephant. She glowed—no, she *burned*—with barely contained excitement.

Again that afternoon she was missing from the home-bound bus. And again the next day. Late in the week I finally flagged her down in a between-class sprint. "Hi, stranger—how's life in the limousine class? I hear you've got a private chauffeur now."

Her unnaturally bright eyes brushed over and past me. Her quick laugh was a tinkling shower of crystal fragments. "Limousine? That wreck? Billy holds it together with bobby pins!"

"You're looking mighty pert these days. Haven't you lost some more pounds?"

"Yes." Her searching gaze found its target. "Well—be seeing you!"

She darted off. Bewildered, I watched her steamroller progress, till Billy McNamara's appearance at the far end of the hall explained her forward charge.

I hadn't known Kay was watching, too, till she spoke beside me. "Wonder if Billy knows the voltage in that wire he's picked up?"

169

"What does *that* mean?"

"Never touch a power line unless you're a qualified electrician."

I gave that one up; Kay's explanations were often more complex than the original puzzle. "Has he asked her for a date yet?"

"Not that she's mentioned—and I'm sure she would."

"With trumpets," I agreed.

The week ended; another one passed—with no announcement from Debbie of a happy event. Yet when I phoned her house, she was never home.

"Debbie? I don't know *where* she is!" Mrs. Fuller's voice grew more fretful by the day. "She said something about going to the library, but my goodness, the library's surely closed by now! It does beat all, the way I never can lay hands on *either* of those girls anymore! I was telling Pa just yesterday—here I've raised two daughters, given them the best years of my life, and where are they when there's work to be done? Off lallygagging with some boy, if you ask me! Leaving *me* to wash and clean and cook and mend and —TOM! WHERE D'YOU THINK YOU'RE GOING, YOUNG MAN? NO, YOU'RE NOT—NOT TILL THOSE DISHES ARE DONE. I DON'T CARE *WHAT'S* ON TEEVEE—"

I put down the receiver softly and made no more calls to the Fuller house. Let Debbie tell me what was going on when she was good and ready.

At the end of the second week, on a Saturday afternoon when (in despair at the day's heavy length) I had just turned out my entire room for wholesale cleaning, Debbie phoned. Not from home. There was no echo of loud Fuller voices in the background, no thump of heavy Fuller footsteps. Instead, a blurred babel punctuated with occasional giggles or guffaws. Pete's, maybe?

"Ellen!" Debbie's voice, high, tense, sent shock-waves down my spine like an electric current. "Do you want to go on a double date tonight?"

"Honest, Debbie! *Really?*"

"Really! We're going to a drive-in . . . the Emerald, I think."

"You're sure you want someone else along? I mean, wouldn't you and Billy rather—"

"It's *got* to be double"—she was too excited to bother with tact—"because it's this other guy's car. Billy's down to three tires, and Barney won't let us use his car unless we get him a date!"

"Barney?"

"Barney Ullman. You don't know him—he's a friend of Billy's. Will you come? Say you'll come!"

"Oh, Debbie . . ." I hesitated. "Me? Shouldn't you get somebody more—more—"

Debbie's voice sank to a low, frantic murmur. "I don't *know* anybody else! Except Kay, and she wouldn't do at *all*. Please, Ellen, they're *waiting!*"

"Well . . . well, sure . . . I guess."

"Oh, good! Ellen, has Mom called?"

"No. Does she think you're here?"

"I didn't *exactly* say that's where I was going, but—if she does call, tell her I'm at the library. Okay?"

It didn't sound like the library to me, but I promised dubiously, "Okay."

"Swell! We'll pick you up around seven thirty. G'bye!"

I went back upstairs to face the tumultuous confusion of my room. Suddenly it hit me. I had a date (even though

171

blind), a real date—my very first! Oh, my goodness, what should I say—how should I act—what was I to wear? How could I *find* anything to wear in this mess? Distractedly I began scooping things up by the armload and stuffing them into the closet. . . .

"Ellen!" cried Mother, passing my open door. "What are you doing?"

What I was doing at the moment was drop-kicking shoes onto the bed to clear space in front of the dressing table.

"Mother, d'you know what? I've got a *date!*" Spoken aloud the words were even more incredible. "A double date with Debbie and Billy! For the show!" Belatedly I remembered to put up a guard of nonchalance. "I was just wondering what to wear."

"Ach, *susel!*" Not at all fooled, Mother threaded her way joyfully through the litter. "We must see now what you have!" Before I could protest, she opened the closet door, and was promptly inundated with tumbling boxes and ballooning crinolines and wadded dresses unfolding like accordions.

I braced myself for her outraged scream, but she wasted no valuable minute on diatribe. With a sturdy heave-ho of shoulder to door she successfully re-bottled the genie, and pronounced, "The new dress—yes, now comes the time for it!"

Aloof above the cyclonic confusion, there it still dangled from the lamp arm where I had hung it that first dreadful week of the diet. "Oh, golly, I don't know. The last time I tried it on—" I didn't finish, not wanting to say when or why that was.

Mother said firmly, "Now is different!" as though she could not only have finished my sentence but glibly recited every measurement on my closely guarded list. How do mothers always *know?*

As soon as she left (which she did with tactful speed), I stripped off shirt and pedal-pushers and slid gingerly into the rustling red charmer. Holding my breath, I inched the zipper upward—past smooth hipline and narrow waist and snugly fitted bodice—to the top! I took an experimental breath—and a deeper one; no seam squeaked a warning. I spun around before the mirror, watching the pleated skirt swirl out and settle gracefully along lines that were curves, not bumps. That was *me*—in a size twelve dress again—and this time minus jutting collarbones and mustard skin and stringy arms. *Me!*

In a state of mild delirium I eased out of my glory and triumph and plunged into a myriad of getting-ready details. A quick hair-set with spray. A bath, instead of the usual shower (so I could luxuriate in skin-smoothing bath oil and a mountain of perfumed bubbles). Ten minutes enforced idleness under a creamy face mask and eye-pads soaked in special lotion ("For a radiant complexion and sparkling eyes," the ad had guaranteed). Fresh polish on my nails—such a heavenly new shade of silver pink I had to touch up my toenails, too.

Dinner in an old bathrobe, with my hair still in rollers (Dad said, "If her young man could see her now!" and the possessive phrase provided more glow than the face mask).

Finally, the painstakingly applied cosmetics. Faintly pink foundation, a whisper of blue eye-shadow, lipstick in twin-shade to my nail polish, a fluff of powder, a touch of new Christmas perfume (like the cool clean scent of woods in winter) on ears and wrists. Off came the rollers—a quick brush—sweet joy! The casual swirls fell into perky place, not a contrary strand to spoil the effect.

Into the dress again. If I'd thought it beautiful with sneakers and tousled hair and shiny nose, now I'd have to call it sensational!

A car swung into the driveway, horn tooting. I gave a last scared glance at the mirror, wishing I could carry it along for reassurance.

"Hold on, princess!" called Dad from the living room as I ran down the stairs. "He's not at the door yet. Let's have a look at you."

I stepped to the entrance, turned gravely once around to show off the dress, then glanced quickly at Dad's face·(Mother's would beam with loving pride, if I wore a size eighteen gunnysack with a string around the middle!). There was no mistaking the genuine admiration in his eyes.

"Well, *well!*" he said. "When did this happen?"

My morale shot up to dizzy heights. I blew them a kiss, and hurried to get my coat from the hall closet just as an impatient rat-a-tat sounded on the front door. Before I could reach it, Debbie flung it open.

"Aren't you *coming?*" she cried. "We've been honking for *ages,* and the guys are getting—" She took a longer look at me. "Good grief, what're you wearing *that* for?"

My brand-new courage crumbled into talcum powder. I looked unhappily at Debbie in a bulky-knit pink turtleneck, a nondescript brief skirt, and an old brown tweed jacket. "You didn't say—I can change in a minute—"

"Do you want to spoil *everything?* Barney's in a snit already! He's some kind of nut about getting to a show on time." Debbie's shrill nervousness completed my rout; I wanted to leap up the stairs and hide under my bed. "Just button your coat and come *on!*"

I crept after her to the driveway where a very old jalopy, painted with bursting rockets, rumbled and shook and emitted clouds of blue smoke. Debbie thrust me in and dived for the back seat.

"Well, here she *is*—at last!" she cried. "Barney, this is Ellen." She giggled self-consciously. "Or is it supposed to be 'Ellen, this is Barney'?"

The leather-jacketed boy, slumped behind the wheel, roared the engine till it backfired. "What's the diff? 'S'long as we get goin'." The car shot into the street while I was still pulling my coat together over my knees; I was caught off-balance and thrown against Barney's arm. Abstractedly, eyes on the road, he pushed me upright. "Later, kid. I'm drivin' now."

Rigid with embarrassment I braced myself against the door so it wouldn't happen again. Billy in the back seat had no such inhibitions.

"Whoops!" he yelled, as the next swooping curve sent him skidding over the worn leather upholstery. "Hey, that was a COD corner for sure!"

"What's a COD corner?"

"Means come over, darling! Barney keeps the seats waxed on purpose."

Debbie squealed in joyous confusion. In contrast to the fun back there, the front seat was a morgue. Why couldn't I think of something to say?

"Uh—I don't remember—have I seen you around Easton?"

"Nope."

"I guess—maybe you've already graduated?"

Billy hooted, "That'd be the day!" And Debbie cried in high-pitched warning, "My goodness, Ellen, did you take Barney for a *schoolboy?*"

"What's wrong with schoolboys?" Billy demanded.

"Well, *nothing!* I just meant—" Hastily Debbie switched subjects. "Barney works for an oil company."

Billy, still disgruntled, said, "She means he's a part-time grease-monkey at a gas station."

Barney spoke in tones of ominous calm. "Pays enough to keep me in wheels, kid. Don't see ya drivin' *your* heap."

"Oh, sure, Barney, I was jus'— Yeh, we're plenty glad the ol' Rocket's still burstin' in air—like the song says—absolutely!"

"Then cut out the cracks about my job."

"Yeh, Barney, sure. Wish I had it myself—could really use the dough."

The tension eased. Barney flipped negligently across traffic to the drive-in approach. "Might speak to the boss about it. But ya gotta lot to learn yet, kid—an' I don't mean that pap at school."

"Yeh, that's right, Barney. Sure be glad to get outa that dump."

On this note of bonhomie we navigated the dark lanes beyond the ticket booth. Barney chose a slot well to the rear, cut his engine with a final roar, adjusted the speaker on the window, and as the theater's "Welcome" sign flashed on the screen said with satisfaction, "Made it!"

With the air of a businessman now ready to take up the next item on his agenda, he glanced over at me. "Hi, kid. Whatcha doin' way over there?"

I tried for an easy laugh that failed abjectly. "Oh, look, a Magoo cartoon! I just love them, don't you? He's so *funny!*"

"Yeh, well, you're pretty funny, too, kid. C'mon over and be friendly."

"Oh, but then Debbie and Billy can't see the screen!"

"Who's lookin'?"

I half turned to enlist support from the rear, then hastily faced forward again. In the silent back seat the two shadowy figures had become one. I protested, "Well, *I* certainly don't want to miss Mr. Magoo—he's my very favorite character! *Please* turn up the sound, Barney; I can hardly hear him!"

"Well, quit yakkin' so much, you'll hear a lot better." Barney's tone was good-humored, as though this preliminary skirmish was just part of the ritual, time-taking but unavoidable. "C'mon, kid, let's get cozy."

What would Ann Landers or Helen-Help-Us advise *now?* While I racked my brains, Barney grabbed my arm and pulled me over to him. I just had time to remember Billy's crack about the waxed seat before my nose was flattened against Barney's jacket. I struggled to get a breath. Barney held me tighter. He nuzzled my neck with his nose and lips like a friendly horse.

"Hey, you smell nice!" he said appreciatively.

I got my head turned just in time to collide bruisingly with his nose. Aggrieved, he jerked upright. I escaped to the far side of the seat, this time keeping a hand behind me in anchor-grip on the door handle. That waxed leather was no joke.

"What's goin' on?" Barney complained, rubbing his nose.

A harried sidelong glance at the back seat brought me no reassurance. Now the single shadow had melted out of sight someplace below the flickering light from the screen. I said the first thing that came into my head.

"We haven't even had our popcorn yet!"

"Who said anything about popcorn?"

"Why, we *always* have popcorn when we go to a drive-in! *Don't* we, Debbie?" (*Where are you, Debbie? Come out of it. Come up for air. SAY something!*) "Popcorn and—and hot dogs and coke—it's practically the best part of the show!"

"Aw, for Pete's sake!" Disgustedly Barney now addressed the back seat. "Thought you said she's on a diet! Okay, fork over back there—it's my wheels an' gas; food's on you."

"Gosh, who wants ta eat?" Billy reared into view. Debbie popped up beside him, hands fluttering ineffectually over wildly disordered hair.

"Yes," she chimed in breathlessly, "who on earth wants to eat?"

"Your girl-friend, that's who. C'mon—give!"

There were scrabbling, clinking sounds as Billy searched for and transferred a handful of coins to Barney. "Thass all I got," he said sullenly.

"Then that's all she eats." Barney slammed the car door so hard the speaker bounced off.

I replaced it with great care, saying apologetically, "Golly, I didn't mean he should get stuff just for me. Isn't anyone else hungry?"

There was no answer. I looked cautiously around. The two-in-one shadow was again sinking below the horizon.

Barney returned with popcorn and a hot dog and two Cokes. I ate very slowly (finding it difficult to swallow even those minute morsels), and took such tiny sips of Coke, the last sliver of ice had time to melt. Popeye followed Mr. Magoo, then a newsreel, then ads, then pre-vues. Two full-length features stretched ahead of us, as interminable and tricky to maneuver as the maze of the Minotaur.

And Barney's grip on my arm was stronger than mine on the door handle.

I tried frantic conversation. "Isn't it heavenly, having it dry for a change! Did you ever try watching a movie between wiper swipes? It's the weirdest—"

I tried intense interest in the screen. "Will you *look* at that house—I never saw anything so spooky! Golly, she's going in! Oooh, I wouldn't dare—"

I tried enormous preoccupation. "Now where did that button go? I heard it hit the floor—anyway, I *think* I heard it. Grief, I've just got to find it—maybe it went down behind the seat—"

And when all else failed, I tried the feminine equivalent of a right to the jaw.

"Wummmph!" said Barney in hurt surprise. "What'd ya do that for?"

I was close to wretched, nervous, childish tears. My best shoes had been trod on, my dress was rumpled, the button that had torn off my coat had taken a piece of material with it—what would Mother say? I wailed, "Just leave me alone, that's all!"

"Well, of all the wild—*okay*, if that's the way you want it! You're not such a treat I'm gonna bust out cryin' about it. I c'd drive down Main right now an' pick up a snappier number, first block." His pride was outraged. I could hear it more strongly in each risingly vehement word. "Come right down to it, I was doin' you a favor—showin' you a real cool time. Felt sorry for you, that's all—"

Abruptly he kicked the starter and gunned the engine. "Sure not gonna waste the whole night on a dumb movie I seen a'ready!"

Billy yelled, "Hey, where you *goin'*?"

"Gonna take baby here back to her mamma, that's where I'm goin'!"

"Wait just a cotton-pickin' minute—I didn't pay a buck a ticket for *nothin'!*"

Barney flung open the door. "Okay—get out then!"

"Aw, for the luvva—gee, Barney, have a heart! I been took

179

for every nickel I got. What'm I gonna *do* if we pull outa here?"

"That's your tough luck," growled Barney, racing the engine till he roused a chorus of protesting horn-blasts from surrounding cars. "Maybe next time you'll get me a date that's outa kindergarten!"

Debbie spoke up quickly. "Gee, that's not it, Barney—I guess Ellen's just kind of upset. It was that hot dog, I bet . . . was it the hot dog, Ellen? Honestly, some of the food they put out at these drive-ins'd kill an ox—and Ellen's got this kind of nervous stomach!" She was giving me an out; every eager word begged me to take it. "But she gets over it awfully fast. Probably she's feeling better already . . . are you, Ellen? Are you feeling better?"

What I was feeling was crushed by misery. Everybody's misery. I wanted to bawl like the baby Barney thought me. For my own disappointment. For Debbie's pathetic anxiety. For Billy's financial embarrassment. Even for Barney's wounded pride.

"Yes," I mumbled, "I'm feeling lots better." I couldn't go home yet; how could I face the folks' surprise at the early hour, their indignation when I explained the reason, their carefully unspoken pity? Oh, how dreadful! "Look, I didn't want Billy to pay for the food; I was going to buy it myself—honest! That's what I always do! Isn't it, Debbie?"

"Oh, sure!" Debbie agreed, treading on the heels of my words. "Ellen always comes *loaded*"—she squealed at the unintentional double-entendre— "Golly, I didn't mean— *You* know what I mean!"

Billy haw-hawed; Barney took his foot off the accelerator; the tension eased ever so little. I dipped hurriedly into my purse. My fingers closed on a bill that I shoved into Billy's hand. "Let's *everybody* have Cokes, what do you say? Except me, that is. Honestly, with this stomach I oughtn't to eat *ever!*"

"Oh, your stomach's not so bad," Barney said gruffly, reaching for the ignition key but not turning it. " 'Course it's pretty dark in here—but I thought it was kinda cute."

I shrilled, louder than Debbie, "Did you hear what he said? Oh, isn't he *terrible?*"

The key turned. The engine lapsed into ear-stunning silence, filled immediately by our relieved jabbering. The crisis was past. Quickly the chatter sloped down once more to murmurs. The dim-lit figures in the back seat again blended into one and were lost in shadow. Barney put his arm tentatively around my shoulders; I made myself go limp and unresisting. He pulled me close. My nose smashed against cool leather, but this time I was no novice; I managed to keep one nostril free for air.

"I meant what I said," he muttered against my ear, "about you bein' kinda cute."

I had exhausted my repertoire of words—and myself. All I could come up with was a feeble "Gee . . . thanks." It seemed to be enough. Barney kissed my ear and neck, reminding me again (in spite of my determined effort to keep my mind blank) of a nuzzling horse searching for a hidden sugar cube. Then he grabbed my chin, pivoted it firmly out of his jacket, and kissed my mouth. A slurpy kiss that first sucked up my persimmon-puckered lips, then let them go with an audible pop. My hands balled into tight fists against his chest; I thought hard about Debbie—and left them there.

"Well," said Barney with satisfaction, "you taste good, too." Like a kid settling down with a sack of peanuts, he shifted to a more comfortable position and prepared to—at last—enjoy the show.

Mother was in bed when I got home but not asleep. She called softly as I tiptoed past her door, "Is it you, Ellen? Did you have a good time?"

"Just marvelous."

"I'm so glad, *susel!* Come tell us about it."

"Tomorrow. It's awfully late, and I'm *dead!*" I yawned in loud proof. "G'night!"

Once in my room I ripped off the red dress and threw it behind the cascading jumble in my closet. It could stay there till it fell apart from hoary old age. A bad-luck dress, bought for a boy who hadn't shown up, worn for a—

Ugh. Late as it was, I went down to the bathroom and stood under a stinging shower till every trace of the evening—perfume, kisses, tears—was washed away.

Twenty-six

Debbie said in aggrieved tones, "Golly, you sure about laid a bomb Saturday night! Almost blew up the whole works."

I'd had a day to simmer down and straighten out my perspective. But it still seemed that I was the one who had a right to feel aggrieved. Debbie's attack—where I'd expected apology—temporarily spiked my guns.

I sputtered, "Well, I like that—after all it cost me!" I hadn't been going to mention the money, but now, caught off guard, it was my first line of defense. "I didn't know till I emptied my purse yesterday—that was a five-dollar bill I handed over for those Cokes!"

"So how was Billy to know? It was dark."

"He'd know when he paid for them! I didn't see him offering me any change."

"He probably never unfolded your stupid bill! They probably gypped him at the refreshment stand!"

"Oh, sure—that's what they do all the time!"

"How would you know? You never went there before. You never had a date to take you!"

"Well, if Barney's a sample, I never want another, either!"

"The way you carried on, that shouldn't be hard to arrange!"

This wasn't the way I wanted it at all. What were we doing squared away here before our lockers, jostled by hurrying kids, yelling at each other like a couple of preschoolers? None of this was what I'd planned to say to Debbie when I saw her again.

"I'm sorry," I said unhappily, wondering how come it was I who'd got backed into the apology corner.

"Well, I should think so!" Only slightly mollified, Debbie whammed her locker door open and began getting out books for her Monday morning classes.

I couldn't leave it like this. Debbie was too hard to pin down nowadays; who knew when I'd get another chance to share yesterday's long sober thoughts? "Debbie, please! You *know* it's not right. All that—that smooching and gobbling—"

"Well, if you mean Barney's a creep"—Debbie hoisted her armload of books into position and backed against the locker door to shut it—"I won't fight about *that*. He is kind of gruesome. But golly, you have to start somewhere."

"I don't mean—I wasn't talking just about Barney. I meant—" I took my courage in my hands and got the words out—"you and Billy, too. I just don't believe a girl has to do all that heavy necking to get a date; and if she does, maybe she's after the wrong guy."

Debbie whirled on me, her cheeks very red. "You better watch out what you're saying!"

"Debbie—where's the difference? If all that steamy carrying on makes Barney a creep, why not—"

"Shut *up!*"

"—why not Billy, too? What's different about it?"

"Just about everything, that's all!" The buzzer sounded for class; we both ignored it, facing each other in the fast-emptying hall like two boxers in a ring. Debbie's voice was shot through with a sort of angry triumph as she delivered a one-two to the ribs. "Billy and I are going steady, that's what's different! He asked me Saturday night!"

"Oh, Debbie, *no*—we've said it a million times—you've said it yourself! What's going steady but swapping necking privileges for a sure date? Look how many steadies some kids have had . . . it's like musical chairs!"

"You don't know anything about it! It's not like that at all! Billy and I—" Debbie balanced delicately in mid-sentence, then let go with her KO punch, "we're in love!"

"Who are you kidding?"

"It's true—we're terribly in love! We'll probably get married right after graduation. As soon as Billy gets a job. So there!"

She meant it. She believed it. Helplessly, even as I went down for the count, I launched a last flurry of jabs. "You just *want* to be in love! You want to so much, you can't wait to be sure that's what it is. You latched onto the first boy who came close enough. Now you're pretending this is it, the genuine twenty-four-carat gold ring! Debbie, *don't!*" I put out a hand pleadingly. "Love's too important. Don't fool yourself about it!"

"*Well!*" said Debbie. The fury disappeared from her voice, to be replaced by a tone of tolerant pity. "I must say, you're a fine one to talk about people fooling themselves. *After Norris!*"

She turned deliberately and walked away from me, head high, shoulders and hips switching ever so slightly. Utterly numb I watched her go.

When a corner cut her off from sight, I moved automatically—some inner mechanism piloting me to the principal's office for a late-slip; to my first-hour class to present it. Like any other day, I took notes, answered questions, and recorded the next day's assignment.

Still operating without conscious volition, I halted Ann Allison after class and asked, "Did you ever get anyone for your Junior Achievement company?"

At the day's end, when the shock of Debbie's low blow had at last worn off, I was appalled to realize that I had not only signed up for Junior Achievement, but for G.A.A. and Y-Teens. I had asked Pat how to become a Peppermint Stick, and under her cheerfully voluble guidance, had volunteered to work six hours a week at the hospital. I had combed the ads in the school weekly and the city daily and had written—and mailed—three letters of application for part-time work.

For twelve dreadful hours I'd been running like a mechanical rabbit from the sound of Debbie's voice—"You're a fine one to talk about people fooling themselves." Out of sheer animal instinct I'd padded myself against the pain of her thrust, cramming every present and future hour with so much activity I'd have no free moment (I hoped) to examine my wound.

Only now the rabbit had run down. Hunched in fierce concentration over an open text, I sat at the desk in my room, fists pressed hard against my ears but silencing nothing, for the voice was inside me.

A fine one to talk about people fooling themselves. After Norris.

How could she throw that at me—when she knew better than anyone how truly I'd cared, how badly I'd been hurt? How could she say—

And not in anger. Not yelling, grabbing for any weapon that would hurt. I could have shaken red-hot, sputtering, angry words out of my head with one brisk flap. No, it was the way she'd spoken—that tone of maternal indulgence for a child's fancied hurt—that drew blood like a cat's claws.

A fine one to talk about people fooling themselves. After Norris.

After Norris.

I knew Debbie and I would never be friends again. Not like before. Not ever.

Twenty-seven

I wish I were a good liar.

I wish I could say that Debbie's taunt projected me into instant triumph. That I went forward and upward to one social success after another, stepped into the role of class leader, forgot shyness and inhibitions and the traumas of self-consciousness, and—merely incidentally—was united with my true love. It would make such a tidy ending to this groping and pretty woebegone recital. I like tidy endings. Heroines in my favorite books always round off their problems neatly, one by one, to emerge like Cinderella in a final climactic blaze of glamor that even their worst enemy has to recognize.

But that isn't what happened.

To begin with I went completely chicken. All I could think of, the morning after that abysmal Monday, was how to get out of the alarming commitments I'd made. Virtually in a state of panic, I searched the halls for Ann Allison while I rehearsed my alibi.

Ann, how lucky I ran into you! You haven't said anything to Roger yet? About JA? Oh, good! Because something's come up—a steady baby-sitting job on Tuesday nights, just too good to pass up—

All of which was no help at all when Roger Austen spoke behind me.

"Hi, Ellen . . . real good to hear you're coming in with us! Did Ann tell you where we meet?"

"No. As a matter of fact—" I strangled on my hurried attempt to rearrange the alibi for other ears. "I was just going to—"

"Well, that's all right, I'll pick you up on my way. It's kind of hard to find, first time—top floor of a warehouse on East Fifth. See you."

Just once (I assured my shaky nerves). I'll get through it somehow, then say this baby-sitting thing came up—only that would sound awful, as though I hadn't liked them—oh, dear—

The Peppermint Sticks needed something different in excuses. "Gee, Pat, I don't know what got into me yesterday —thinking I could scrape up free time after school, with all that's going on this last semester—"

"Isn't it the truth?" she assented cheerily. "I'm run absolutely *ragged!* But that's what they always say: when you want something done, go to the busiest person you know. Oh, yes, just ask for Nurse Duncan this afternoon; she's the one in charge of volunteers."

"Won't you be there, too?" Shock jolted excuses clear out of my mind.

"Not me. I bat out my whole week's quota on Saturday. Tougher on me, but easier on the family wheels."

"Ulp—oh, golly—" *Me*, go alone to that hospital—tackle unfamiliar work—with strangers? Never! I just wouldn't show up—

"Nurse Duncan thinks you sound just fine for the children's ward. I phoned her last night, told her all about you. She'll be looking for you."

Trapped. "Thanks," I said hollowly.

Pat was in G.A.A., too. "Hey, where are you going?" she shouted, when at the beginning of activity period I tried to sneak unobtrusively to the library. "Choosing up sides for volley ball today! Got you earmarked for my team."

And Ann Allison—wouldn't you know it?—turned out to be a shining light in Y-Teens. "How nice you've joined, Ellen! We can drive in together."

I was encircled, hemmed in, the net drawn tighter at every turn. No choice but to stumble through one ghastly experience, only to collide with another. A snail without its shell, an unfledged bird fallen from the nest, naked, shivering . . .

Here's another place for a tidy wrap-up. I can see exactly how it should read: *Forcibly ejected from her cocoon of shyness, Ellen Frazer startled herself more than anyone by emerging as Girl Butterfly. In Junior Achievement, her deft fingers were invaluable in fashioning clever items for sale; her splendid marketing suggestions put Westco Products out front as top JA profit-earner for the year. . . .*

Hah!

I wove out of my first JA meeting, my face set in the glazed smile I'd pasted on when the doorbell announced

Roger, my ears buzzing with a confusion of undigested facts and figures. Get out and sell that stock—have to raise capital —production starts Saturday—let's everybody show up— workers earn twenty-five cents an hour—Westco stock paid sixteen percent last year on gross earnings of $334.02 after/ before/during (?) taxes—cash on hand, inventory, assets, salaries, commissions—Mr. Chairman, I rise to a point of information—Mr. Chairman, how do I get out of this mess?

"Enjoy it, Ellen?" Roger asked, when he dropped me home afterward.

I gave him a slightly stretched version of The Smile. "Great."

Dad met me at the door. "Well, Ellen, how'd it go?"

"Splendid." I staggered for the stairs—so much yet to do (up, down, brush, scrub, mend, press), but conscience stopped me. Dad was an Opportunity To Be Seized. Put back The Smile; widen it with fresh young enthusiasm; recharge that apathetic voice. "Hey, Dad, want to get in on a real gilt-edged investment? Westco Products paid a sixteen percent dividend last year; just take a look at this prospectus! Sorry we've got a limit per customer; can't sell you more than five shares—"

Five more to Mother, five to myself. Two to Mrs. Markey next door. Two to the milkman. One to the school janitor. One to the bus driver. One to the drycleaner. So they went, each sale a teeth-gritting effort with an aftermath of moist palms and rumbling stomach. But, come Saturday, I could present myself at the JA workroom with modest pride; I had sold all my shares.

So had everybody else.

No heroine, just a twenty-five-cents-an-hour peon, I spent a wretched, fumbling afternoon at the glue pot, trying to fit strips of red felt to obnoxious double-right-angled bits of black metal. I got glue on my skirt, and glue in my hair. The felt stuck to my gluey fingers and to stray papers and to the table. When it stuck to the metal, it was more often than not crooked or wrinkled; to get it off and start over again left me and my entire surroundings in a bright red fuzz.

"Everything going all right?" (Our production adviser. Friendly, alert, frighteningly efficient.)

Give him The Smile, the original, one and only Red-Felt Smile. "Just fine, Mr. Samuels. But I can see why they're only paying me twenty-five cents an hour—ha, ha!" (A joke, a real live red-felt joke! Must have sniffed too much glue.)

"Worth every penny of it," he assured me. (Did I see a twinkle as he turned away, or was it just the fuzz on my eyelashes?)

Or take the Peppermint Sticks, fiction versus fact: *Ellen Frazer, Girl Butterfly, revealed a sure instinct for healing. Her very appearance at the entrance to the children's ward had a calming effect on the restless young patients. Her gentle touch cooled fevered brows. There were unashamed tears in Nurse Duncan's eyes as she pressed Ellen's hand gratefully, and said—*

"Keep moving, Frazer! You won't get around the entire ward if you dally so long at every bed."

"But they want to see all the books before they choose—"

"Nonsense. Just give each one a book, and keep moving."

"Yes, ma'am."

"I do' *want* Bo-Peep! I a'ready *had* Bo-Peep!"

"Shhh, here's another."

"I do' want Three Bears! I had Three Bears yestiddy! I wanna *see* the books!"

"Shhh, the nurse will hear you if—"

"*I wanna see the books!*"

"Shut *up!*"

Startled silence. Big accusing eyes. Underlip thrust out.

"Don't cry! Tell you what, I'll be back if I have time. *Please* don't cry! The nurse will—okay, okay, *look* at the books then!"

"You *yelled* at me!"

"No, I didn't, I only said—"

"Yes, you did so yell! An' I'm *sick!*"

"I'm sorry!" I was more than sorry; I was dewy with nervous perspiration, and shaking with panic. If the little monster kept this up, he'd bring Nurse Duncan on the run. I tumbled books all over the bed. "There! Look at all the nice books!"

"I do' wanna look at the books! I wanna go *home!*"

A sympathetic sniffle from the next bed. A tearful hiccough from the next. The monster had said that word, and now contagion spread faster than the plague. "*I wanna go home!*"

"Frazer, what's going on here?"

"Nothing, ma'am, I just—" I braced myself for the monster's stern accusation, "She *yelled* at me!" but unbelievable silence gripped the entire ward.

"Well, keep that cart moving!" Nurse Duncan's cold eye assessed the litter on the monster's bed. "And remember, *only one book* to a child!"

"Yes, ma'am."

Smart tattoo of rubber heels retreating. Faint stir in the silent ward. Grins passing from bed to bed like a wordless countersign. The monster winked at me.

I winked back.

Then there was volleyball: *Ellen Frazer, Girl Butterfly,*

193

*turned out to be a natural athlete, possessing the coordina-
tion, the swift reactions, the mental agility of a champion. In
the all-important G.A.A. finals, her vigorous attack under
great odds rallied her entire team. Point by crucial point,
they fought to a 13–13 tie, then inched ahead 14–13. A perfect service—back came the ball—another volley, and another—a whopping strike by the opposition, going over their
heads, out of everyone's reach—except Ellen's! Like a mountain cat, she sprang upward, the heel of her hard-muscled
fist connecting powerfully with the ball . . .*

Just as my feet went out from under me, bringing down
with me the only player in position to have salvaged my
weak tap and kept the ball in the air. Gleefully the opposing
team took the serve and the next three points to win.

"Oh, well," said Pat philosophically, "there's always another game. Next time—"

Next time, I'd foozle it again. The approach of any moving
object—ball, bird, puck—seemed to paralyze me. Immobile
as a bird before a snake, I'd watch it come, till—off-balance,
out of position, hopelessly late—I flailed at it gracelessly and
quite often disastrously.

Ellen Frazer, high-point scorer—for the other team. Ellen
Frazer, kiss of death—for any captain luckless enough to
take me on. Pat, who most often volunteered for the burden,
must have been piling up brownie points that spring like
confetti.

In some ways Y-Teens was my worst nightmare. My vocabulary rebels at presenting even a fictional portrait of
Ellen Frazer, inspirational leader, public-spirited goodfellow
—nope, it just wasn't in me.

Grimly, like facing up to a dental appointment, I fulfilled
the very minimum of public duties. I sold programs at the

basketball tournament (or rather, I held a stack of them and let spectators force money on me, if they so desired).

I served at the father-son banquet (but cravenly in the kitchen, filling trays instead of passing them).

I raised money for the crippled children's school (not like the others, by selling homemade cookies and candy, but by buying them—all my own wares that I'd prepared so painstakingly, then hadn't the nerve to peddle. It cost me two weeks' pay, and I couldn't even eat the stuff—not on my diet. I left most of it in the JA workroom, when nobody was around, with an anonymous sign saying, "Help yourself!" But first I made up a little box of the nicest pieces for Mr. Appleby).

Mr. Appleby was my boss ("Salesgirl, Saturdays 9:00–1:00, some typing"). His was the only answer to my application letters; till it came, I was keeping my fingers crossed that employers would be unanimous in not wanting me. But there it was, with an hour set for an interview like a command—BE THERE.

I found the address with difficulty, a little stationer's shop off the main street on a sort of dead-end alley. I had almost more trouble finding Mr. Appleby. The dim shop seemed empty. I stood at the counter uncertainly, wondering how long I must wait before I dared cut and run. To prove to myself that I was really trying, I called softly, "Is anybody in?"

A voice above me answered, "Up here."

Nerves shattered, I spun wildly around to see a pale moon rising out of a suspended birdcage. My vision cleared; the moon became a round, expressionless face, the birdcage a small grille-fronted office reached by an almost invisible stairway at the back of the shop. I groped my way up, already so demoralized that the interview couldn't add more to my terror—I thought.

The rest of Mr. Appleby was as round as his face. After letting me in, he barricaded himself instantly behind his desk, scrabbled through an immense drift of papers, frowned portentously, and barked, "Ellen Frazer?"

I admitted it faintly. "Yes."

"Type?"

"A—little. But slow."

"Selling experience?"

"No."

His frown by now was tremendous, and my voice barely audible. Why didn't he just say I wouldn't do? It was plain he didn't like me.

"Student?"

"Senior. Easton High."

"Age?"

"Seventeen."

"Address?"

"760 Chestnut Road." It was all there in the letter he was holding; he didn't have to make me repeat it in my scared fluttery voice. A sadist, that's what he was. He *liked* seeing his victims suffer.

"Social Security number?"

"I—don't have any."

"Get one. Post office. Go look over the stock. I'll get you a sales pad."

It took me all the way to the foot of the stairs to realize I was hired. But it took me several Saturdays to discover that Mr. Appleby was that rare creature—a person shyer than me. The approach of a customer—fortunately for both of us, they were few—sent him scuttling for the birdcage.

That, he explained later when we'd got past monosyllables, was why he had needed a Saturday clerk. His regular mainstay (a domineering bully, I was convinced) had refused to work more than a five-day week; he had either to wait on customers himself till Saturday's one o'clock closing, or hire more help. The choice must have been frightful. Mine was the first answer to his ad; that's why I got the job. I think he would have hired a zombie with ten thumbs and a furry tail, to avoid more interviews.

You can see we were made for each other.

I put the box of goodies on his desk when I was left in temporary possession of the birdcage to type a letter (the office was too small for two to work in at the same time). Naturally he didn't thank me. That would have been too embarrassing for both of us. But in my next pay envelope I found my check folded around a delicate, snowy Madeira handkerchief.

"Don't move!" A firm, freckled hand pinned me against my locker. "Where have you *been?* I never see you anymore."

"Oh, hi, Kay. What's up?"

"The Tergles are up—for sale, that is. Come on home with me and see them while they're still a whole family. Any day now they'll be snapped up—prrrt, prrrt, prrrrt!"

"Are they that old *already?* Isn't possible!"

"Two months and ten days." Kay's voice was wistful; her angular face already looked bereaved. "Seems awfully young to kick 'em out of the nest—but if I don't, Midge will. She's getting pretty bored with motherhood. Anyway, Ed says puppies should find homes while they're still little and cute —crossbreeds, especially."

"Ed?"

"The boy at the vet's."

My thoughts flipped back to New Year's Eve—a lifetime ago. "The stupid idiot?"

"What do you mean, stupid idiot?" Kay flared. "What's stupid about an Aggie soph, studying veterinary medicine?"

I said meekly, "I was only quoting you."

"Oh. Oh, then! I guess I was kind of upset that night—imagine not knowing when a dog's in whelp!"

"You're beginning to sound like a vet yourself." I looked at my watch. "Oh, golly, I've got to tear!"

"You mean you're *not* coming home with me?"

"Not now." I gave the balance of my day a quick mental run-down. The hospital now. JA tonight—an extra shift to speed up production of our over-the-door hangers before Saturday's sale. But I didn't have to be there by any specific hour. "How about tonight?"

"Why, uh—" For a barely perceptible moment Kay hesitated. "Fine! Ed'll be there, too. He's going to help me decide which Tergles are worth most—you know, best conformation and all that."

Suddenly I felt oppressed by unreasoning sadness, a wave of heavy melancholy that Mother would have called *weltschmerz*. It took real effort to say lightly, "Wouldn't think of interrupting a business conference! Let's make it tomorrow night, huh? Don't sell anything till I get there! See you!"

First Debbie, now Kay—each finding her own way into a world we'd all set out to enter. Only I had come up against a blank wall. . . .

Twenty-eight

A low, low day.

New faces in the hospital ward, but with the same old problems.

"I do' want that book! I a'ready had that book! . . . I wanna see *all* of 'em!"

A wail from the next bed. "I won't *ever* get to pick a book! He's alla time lookin' at 'em!"

"Aw, who cares about th' ol' books? I seen 'em all, ain't any there good as teevee. I wanna go—"

I forestalled the word with inspiration born of despair. "How about if I *tell* you a story?"

"YAY!"

"What about? Is it about—"

"Shuddup an' let 'er tell it!"

"Be quiet now, all of you. . . . Once upon a time there was a boy—"

"What's his name?"

"Where'd he live?"

"How old is he? Is he big as me?"

"Shhh! . . . His name was Peter, and he was just about your size. He and his little sister, Nancy, lived with their parents and a dog and a horse and a cat and a duck and two parakeets and a turtle and a white rat and two guinea pigs—"

"Gee!"

"—in a little house beside a big river. Now it happened that upriver from Peter and Nancy lived a cross old man who—didn't—like—pets—at—all! They cost good money, he said. And they ate up good food. And they took up good time. *Nobody* should have pets, he said, nobody—at—all!"

"I do' like *him!* He's mean!"

"Now every time the cross old man went to town, he had to pass Peter's and Nancy's house, where he could *plainly* see a horse and a dog and—"

"Duck!" a small voice helped me out.

"Cat!"

"Turtle!"

"Silly, how's he gonna see a *turtle?* . . . He couldn't see the turtle, *could* he?"

"Yes, he could, because it was a *big* turtle, and Peter and Nancy kept it in a pond in their front yard. Of course, every now and then the turtle would get out of the pond to take a walk in the green grass and the flower beds; sometimes, it *even* crossed the road—"

"Ohhh! Where cars went?"

"Bet that mean ol' guy hit it! On purpose!"

"No, *no!*"

"*Shuddup!* Let 'er tell it!"

The story rambled along (at a turtle's pace, naturally), following whatever by-path the children showed interest in, and promising to be as endless as any tale of Scheherazade's. It got me through the hour without yells, tears, or the appearance of Nurse Duncan. And it left me out of breath, and totally out of ideas.

"See you t'morrow!" the children called after me when the appearance of supper trays at last provided release. "Don't fergit!" *Tomorrow?* The prospect dismayed me.

I felt too tired, too dispirited, to cope with a city bus at rush hour. Instead, I phoned Mother that I'd eat downtown, grabbed a rubbery cheese sandwich at the nearest lunch stand, then went on to the JA workroom.

At this early evening hour the big room echoed with gloomy emptiness. I set out my materials on the Westco table and went mechanically to work. But though my fingers now moved more adeptly, my heart was dragging bottom. Debbie—going steady. Kay—"Ed's coming over." And me? I was on a merry-go-round; the faster I whirled, the quicker I came right back where I'd started.

Ellen Frazer, going nowhere. Ellen Frazer, girl dud.

Last year at this time—

The *weltschmerz* rose up and overwhelmed me. I laid my head down on the cluttered table and wept. Last year there had been Norris' letters to look forward to; I had waked to each day as though it were a Christmas package to be unwrapped. Now what did I have?

Up, down, brush, scrub, don't-eat-that, stand-up-straight,

SMILE. Once-upon-a-time . . . one-thousand-and-one-red-felt-lined-door-hangers . . . dear-sir-in-answer-to-yours-of-the-seventh . . . get-that-ball . . . sell-that-ticket . . . hi-Celia (Pat-Joan-Ben-Amy-Sue-Bob) . . . SMILE.

I couldn't glue another strip of red felt. My tears spotted the very few hangers I had completed. I shoved them well down in one of the boxes we'd be taking out to sell at neighborhood stores Saturday—

Anyway, *somebody* would be taking them out to sell. Not me. I was getting off the merry-go-round. I was going home and *not* brush-scrub-mend-press-up-down-diet-exercise-SMILE.

I was all through improving myself . . . all done pounding on that blank impervious wall. Who wanted in, anyway?

Carefully I erased my name from the sign-in list, so I wouldn't be credited with an hour's work. Even at Westco rates, it would be a gyp. Then I turned off the lights and closed the door on the big room that, for me, was empty even when it hummed with activity.

Nearest bus stop to home was on Lake Boulevard, half a mile from 760 Chestnut Road. I tramped the rest of the way, head down, stubbornly ignoring the sweet scents beginning to fill the air. Soon dogwood would be in bloom, cherry orchards would be frilled out in pink formals, every bush and tree and flower would sing its hymn to spring in colors that blended like a mighty chord. Only in my heart was it still winter.

Mother jumped to her feet at my appearance. "Ellen, what did you have to eat? I kept dinner warm—just in case. Tonight it was veal goulash with dumplings. But then you don't eat veal goulash and dumplings!"

"Oh, yes, I do," I told her hardily. "*And* egg bread, if

you've got it. And fruit salad with lots of sour-cream dressing, and apple strudel and dates and nuts and figs and honey cookies—the whole works!"

"*Liebchen!* Ach, did you hear her, David? The child has come to her senses at last! . . . Sit now, it will take only a minute."

Joyfully Mother bustled out to ransack stove and cupboard and refrigerator. I followed her tiredly, slumped into my place at the kitchen table . . .

And saw, on top of the day's very thin offering of mail, a letter addressed in tall, slanted, distinctive print.

Twenty-nine

Ellen, I miss your letters so much. It's as though a great vacuum-cup had come down around me, shutting off all sound.

Lying restlessly awake, hours later, I heard the phrases repeat themselves, like the top phonograph record when the automatic cut-off doesn't work. I had read Norris' letter so many, many times before I at last turned out the light, that I could recite it almost entirely from memory.

What can I say about Christmas? How explain the coward-ice that kept me from coming? We had created such a beautiful thing in our private world of you-and-me-and-Uncle-Sam

. . . would it stand transplanting? At the last moment, I lost my nerve; I was afraid to find out . . .

I flung myself to the other side of the bed. The sheets were crosshatched with wrinkles, the blanket half on the floor. Why couldn't I find a comfortable position? My head ached sluggishly; my waistline seemed pushed up under my ribs; my stomach was surely the size—and weight—of a watermelon.

Better forget explanations; your understanding heart will have told you the sorry facts long before this. Better just to throw myself on your mercy and say, "Please, Ellen!" See—I am on my knees to you (an uncomfortable position, too, in this hair shirt and on these nettles!); don't I look forlorn enough to rouse your pity? Tell me I'm forgiven, Ellen. Tell me you'll write again.

Drat—there went the pillow! I groped for it in the well of deeper darkness beside the bed and succeeded only in tilting the night stand; my alarm clock hit the floor with a twanging "boing!" With an exasperated sigh I got up and turned on the light. What a mess I'd made of the bed! No wonder I couldn't get to sleep.

The clock, stubbornly durable, was still ticking. Just to be on the safe side I set it this time on the dresser, and—meeting my reflection in the mirror—had to acknowledge that the bed wasn't the only thing in a mess. Rebelliously I'd omitted the usual bedtime ritual. My hair, unbrushed, unset, stiff with yesterday's hair spray, stood out from my head in witches' spikes; my unwashed face felt—and looked—dry and gritty; the shapeless muu-muu I'd dragged from the laundry basket was wrinkled and had a ripped seam under one arm.

Hurriedly I smoothed the bedcovers and turned off the light. Why think about such ridiculous details as a ripped seam and an unwashed face? Norris had written me—Norris had set down those beautiful, pleading words—*Norris!*

And see how wrong I'd been! All those morbid imaginings of why he hadn't come! He *hadn't* seen me and turned tail like a scared rabbit. He *hadn't*—oh, glory, oh, hallelujah!— found a girl who gave him all I'd provided, plus tangibility.

Then why wasn't I afloat on a pink-tinted cloud, nibbling ambrosia and exchanging news-of-the-day with Eros and Hebe?

Other vacations are coming (that's how the letter had ended). *If you give me another chance, who knows?—we may yet meet . . . sometime, somewhere . . .*

He did want to see me; didn't that prove it? *Sometime, somewhere.* Leave it that way. An indefinite magic something in the future. In the meantime there'd be his letters to look forward to again . . . those enthralling, delightful, absorbing letters . . . like talking to my other self, the half that made me whole, a mirror held up to my heart.

An end to loneliness and hungering for communication; an end to hammering on a cold, unyielding wall.

Bliss. And all that stood between me and its enjoyment was my wretched too-full stomach. I wasn't used to eating big meals anymore, but after Mother had gone to the bother of preparing all that food, I'd had to stuff it in somehow. Anyway, reading and re-reading Norris' unbelievable letter, I'd scarcely noticed what or how much I ate.

I groaned aloud. Maybe I should go downstairs for some milk-of-magnesia tablets . . . I could find them in the dark. . . .

Why was I against turning on a light? Was I afraid to meet myself in another mirror? I flopped over on my ballooning stomach and pulled the pillow over my head.

"Count your blessings," I reminded myself. "No more up-down-brush-scrub. No more red felt, or fund-raising, or leaping over a basketball court like an overgrown mongoose."

No more hi-there and SMILE. No more straining invention to keep Peter and Nancy alive. No more cringing at sight of an approaching customer.

I could go back to my own private world. . . .

Suddenly, I sat straight up in bed. The pillow slid again to the floor.

"But what if it doesn't fit any more?" I asked aloud.

Anymore than rich meals fitted my new waistline?

Good grief, of all the silly ideas to come up with! Impatiently my fingers searched and found the pillow and brought it back to bed level. I pressed my hot face into it, and at last fell into troubled sleep.

Thirty

"Terry Turtle was in an awful spot! He was so far from home now that he simply couldn't find his way back. And what's worse—what he *didn't* know—he was in the very yard of the cross—old—man!"

It was the children who had trapped me, of course. I tried to retreat . . . believe me, I tried harder than Terry Turtle! But when Peppermint Stick time rolled around the next day, there I was—back at the hospital—churning out more adventures of the creatures I'd so rashly brought to life.

Because how could you disappoint a kid? A sick kid, at that? Why, I even had to promise one home-visit to each patient about to be dismissed, so the Word wouldn't trigger a new outbreak of tears—"I do' *wanna* go home! How'll I know what *happened?*"

Then there was Mr. Appleby. If I quit my job, he'd be forced back into the marketplace to find another Saturday clerk—poor, nice, shy Mr. Appleby, who fled to his birdcage at the very prospect of an interview! No, I couldn't desert him before our already accepted September-and-college parting. Besides—it was amazing how brave I was getting on Saturday mornings, knowing that he admired my boldness in confronting customers!

And Roger. Roger lived, woke, slept, ate JA. In the big workroom his hesitant shyness was swept away by a tidal wave of enthusiasm. ("We've got a *good* product; it's reasonably priced—now how shall we sell it? We need every idea you can come up with. We need every pair of hands.") How could you go up to someone like that and say "I quit"?

Pat—so generous with her friendship, whacking my shoulder after even my most miserable performance, "Good try, Ellen! You're a real sport!" How was I to meet her loud reproach, "Hey, you mean you'd leave the team *short?*"

Or face Ann's honest surprise—"But Ellen, we were *counting* on you! You never let us down."

What I'd got into was quicksand. I'd stepped recklessly off the narrow, familiar path; now I was gripped by an irresistible force, and the more urgently I flailed and struggled to be free, the more firmly I was held. Terry Turtle might find his way back home, but not me; for good or bad, I was permanently out of my shell.

I went to Kay's house for a last visit with the Tergles— delightful puppies, with the brash, heart-conquering insouciance of young animals confident of love.

"Much better to put a price on them," Kay explained, "even though they aren't purebreds. Kids value a pet more if it costs them a little something; they take better care of it. Besides, the Tergles are pretty special. They've had all their shots; they're practically housebroken . . ."

I looked at the velvety carpet that I used to be scared to step on (the Tergles' invasion obviously hadn't stopped with the back entry), but I didn't contradict her. Not that it would have bothered her if I had; she looked much too cheerfully, competently—what was the word I wanted?—adjusted.

"Next year," she went happily on, "I'm going to give Midge a second go-round with Gay Blade. Ed thinks she'll take him, now she's had a litter. Of course, I'll let her skip a season, or even two—it's a mistake to breed a bitch too frequently—"

"Kay, you're forgetting something. Next year we'll be at State U."

"Not me! I'm staying right here at Western Ag. I'm going to be a D.V.M."

"A *vet?*"

"Sure, why not? I love everything Ed's told me about it—and I've been helping over at the animal hospital. It's something terribly worth doing, Ellen; it takes heart and hands, as well as brains . . ."

"Is it Ed?" I asked.

She followed my thoughts with her usual chain-lightning swiftness. "I don't know, Ellen. If things work out that way—fine. If not—well, maybe there'll be someone else." She gave me a lopsided puckish grin. "No man will ever choose me for my fatal charm, you know. But maybe someday, somebody I'm working alongside—"

She looked down at her long, strong, capable fingers spread wide on her knees. "Anyway, that's how it's got to be, Ellen—the only way it'll happen for me."

So she'd found her door in the wall, I thought, seeing her go with regret, admiring the intelligence that could analyze itself so clearly and wisely. And of course mathematically!

Debbie, now—she hadn't bothered with doors. She'd sailed over the wall on a magic carpet of hope. . . .

I sighed just a little. "Looks like Debbie found what she was after, too."

"Seems so. Guess they're quite a case. She says they're planning to get married right after graduation."

"As soon as Billy gets a job."

"Billy? Oh, that broke up weeks ago, didn't you know? He was just too, too immature, she said—and I must say he's been looking years younger since the split! Always knew she had entirely too much voltage for him to handle. Anybody has, who's way ahead of you in knowing what they want."

"But then who—"

"Oh, this one's already out of school. What's his name now?—Barney something."

Over the wall. And whether she landed safely, or crashed, who could yet know?

It was eight-year-old Lisa at the hospital who, soon afterward, brought me full-circle to the subject of names. Lisa whiled away uncomfortable hours in traction by naming her future children. Three girls and two boys, that's what she was going to have. Each day her list of names varied to allow for new inspiration; each day I must write down her latest decisions.

"Ellen, hey, Ellen, d'you know what I'm going to name my children?" It was her daily greeting, always in the same

211

tone of breathless enthusiasm as though the subject had never been brought up before.

"No! What?" I'd ask, turning her pillow, smoothing her hair back from her flushed, eager face before I took up pencil and pad.

Lisa's children always had beautiful names like Kathleen and Angela and Rosemary, strong names like Steven and Douglas and Lance. So it was the more startling, on this particular afternoon, to hear her say, ". . . And then comes Christine, and next is Michael, and the baby's Ellen!"

Involuntarily my pencil jerked to a halt. "Oh, no, not Ellen! Give her a pretty name."

"It *is* a pretty name!" Lisa leaped to indignant defense.

"But not like Rosemary and Christine . . ."

"Of course not! It's *different* pretty!" Exasperated, she squeezed her eyes tight-shut to concentrate better on an explanation simple enough for my limited understanding. "Rosemary's pretty like flowers, see? And Christine's pretty like a star. But Ellen's pretty like—like *water*, don't you see? Cool and clean."

"Oh." I nodded, and meekly wrote it down.

But she had started me weaving a chain of fanciful thought. Lisa, of course, coupled my name with cool hands and a fresh, crisp uniform; long after the hospital and I were forgotten, "Ellen" would remind her of something pleasantly cool and clean.

What associations might it have for others who knew me?

I could almost guess. "Real sport" (that would be Pat). "Hard-working" (Roger). "Dependable" (Ann). "Strong, brave" (only Mr. Appleby would associate "Ellen" with a sturdy bulwark!).

Mother . . . Dad . . . Miss Heller . . . Mr. Stanton, each would have a different answer.

A name is what you make it.

I read and re-read and re-re-read Norris' letter. In my mind I composed many answers; none of them reached paper. Because what could I say to him that he wanted to hear? *A world composed of just oneself—and a mirror—is too constricting. Come out, come out—*

No, that's something a person has to find out for himself.

At long last—and not without tears—I made a neat package of his picture and the quantities of snapshots, and mailed it to him. Better to stay away from words; the package was answer enough.

As for his letters—oh, those poignantly beautiful letters!— I shredded them to bits on a sunny Saturday afternoon and fed them one by one to the backyard incinerator. It was like pulling my fingernails out by the roots. Yet, as the last one crumbled to gray ash and a fleeting trail of smoke, I knew an immense sense of freedom. There went my private world —my lovely, secret, unreal world. I could never again pretend myself into its rose-tinted shell, dream myself into Elin or Elaine . . . enchanting, witty, delightful, beloved.

For better or worse, I was me.

Mother called from the back door. "The telephone, Ellen!"

"Coming!"

I picked up the receiver. "Hello?"

"Hi," said Roger. "You coming down this afternoon?"

"Pretty quick now. I had something to do here first."

"Oh, well, no hurry. I just got to wondering—I mean, you always do come on Saturday afternoon—"

Something in his voice . . . "Yes," I said, surprised at the soft breathless way the word came out, "yes, I always do."

Silence, but not the separating kind that means you're about to hang up. I waited. . . .

"Wouldn't blame you if you didn't want to come. Almost too nice a day to stay inside."

"Oh, that's all right. I don't mind."

Again the communicating silence. Then Roger spoke diffidently, not in his JA voice at all. "Tell you what—how'd it be if we quit early and had a picnic supper up on the Butte? Do you mind a climb?"

"I'd love it!"

"You would?" Relief erased the diffidence. "Swell! On a day like this, along about sunset, the view up there's terrific. Like looking down on the Promised Land."

"Yes," I said softly. "Like the Promised Land."

In the wall are many doors. Be patient, search with diligence, for one will open to your key. And oh, the land beyond is very fair. . . .

Format by The Etheredges
Set in Linotype Baskerville
Composed, printed and bound by American-Stratford, Inc.
Harper & Row, Publishers, Incorporated